Spirits of the High Mesa

by

Floyd Martínez

Arte Público Press
Houston, Texas
1997

This volume is made possible through grants from the National Endowment for the Arts (a federal agency), Andrew W. Mellon Foundation, the Lila Wallace-Reader's Digest Fund and the City of Houston through The Cultural Arts Council of Houston, Harris County.

Recovering the past, creating the future

Arte Público Press
University of Houston
Houston, Texas 77204-2090

Cover illustration by Consuelo Udave
Cover design by Gladys Ramirez

Martínez, Floyd.
Spirits of the high mesa / by Floyd Martínez.
p. cm.
ISBN 1-55885-198-4 (pbk. : alk. paper)
I. Title.
PS3563.A7333433S68 1997
813' .54—DC21 96-50286
CIP

The paper used in this publication meets the requirements of the American National Standard for Permanence of Paper for Printed Library Materials Z39.48-1984.

Printed in the United States of America

Spirits of the High Mesa

There is a place where the jagged Rocky Mountains gracefully descend to flat mesas of *piñón* and juniper and where the arroyos that drain the snow and the rain are like magic windows for what went underground long ago. Even lower, on the vast plains, *maize* and *calabazas* have for centuries nourished the living and honored the dead. For those who were always there, it was called *P'osoge*; for those who came later, it is *la tierra de poco tiempo;* and for those who have just arrived it is *the land of enchantment.*

PARTE UNA

Beginnings

UNO

We found bones. Big bones. Teeth, too, that must have belonged to monster creatures far bigger than our horses. After the big rains we would go see what things from ancient times were poking out of the deep arroyo where the water had washed away the sandy walls. My brother Juan said they were from dinosaurs, but who knows? Maybe they were just from a big cow that had fallen in the mud and drowned long ago.

Along the rocky slopes at the edge of the *piñón monte* we also found pieces of painted pots scattered all over as if somebody's wife had gotten mad. Perfect arrowheads, too, so sharp they could cut a finger off. On a real lucky day we might find an ax made of fine black stone, no doubt used by some long-dead hunter or maybe just a woodcutter. And along the yellow and red *barrancas,* beyond the deep arroyo, were caves where maybe this woodcutter or hunter had once lived.

If we stood facing north we could see the snow-white peaks of the San Juans, and to the right, the deep forest. Past the Mesa del Frances to the left was the Apache Nation of the Jicarilla, and beyond them, the Navajo. So our village of Capulín was surrounded by all this and by so many groves of chokecherry bushes that no wonder the place was called

Capulín. When we ate the little purple berries our teeth turned brown, and for part of August and all September all of us kids had brown teeth. But by October, they were back to yellow.

In the mail once a week we got two newspapers, one Spanish, one English. They kept us educated about a world I had never seen. They told of wars and crimes, of marriages and cars for sale, but the best part was the funnies in the Sunday ones. In the kitchen my father had a big wooden radio run by a battery that looked like a giant can of Spam. It told stories about *The Shadow,* and *Fibber McGee and Molly*. And *The Lone Ranger,* who was tough because he never lost a fight to the *bandidos;* and Tonto was so much help to him. Tonto spoke such good English, too, not like those we knew who spoke only Indian and Spanish. But I could never figure out why such a smart Indian was called Tonto.

The radio's most important job was to tell the news. Every night, a little before six, my father would turn it on to warm it up. This meant we were all supposed to shut up. We did. Right at six a strong, almost mean voice would say, "Good evening, this is Morgan Beatty with the news." Then Mr. Beatty would go on to tell about the war and how units of the North Korean army had moved south as far as the 38th parallel. I pictured them as little red people with long black braids carrying guns with long pointed knives on the barrel, big pouches of bullets on their shoulders, and *guaraches* on their feet. Almost always there was a story about the president and something important he had said. Sometimes it was so important that the president said it himself. I felt so proud because it sounded as if he were talking to me. At the end came the weather, but we didn't have to listen to that part. My father said that Mr. Beatty was not talking about our weather.

Our school. It stood on top of the little mesa overseeing the valley, with its adobes already rounded off at the corners. Inside, the blackboard with the abc's on top was faded; the potbelly in the corner spit smoke and fire. The desks, each one with a hole for the ink bottle, were arranged so the small ones were in front and the big ones in the back. The shelves on one side of the room served as library, coat rack, storage and the beds for sick or just lazy kids. The schoolyard was almost all tumbleweeds, except this year we had a new bell and a flag-pole for the good ole stars and stripes. Two privies were back along the fence, one for boys and one for girls. And on the other side of the fence, Emilio Sánchez stacked his vega hay and next to it the *corrales* where he kept his precious rams. With no slide, no monkey bars, and no swings, Emilio's rams were what recess was all about.

They were giant wooly monsters with huge curl horns and yellow eyes that saw everything. And below hung big *huevos*. The game was to sneak into the pen and run from one side to the other without death. The close calls got cheers. If you were really brave you stopped in the middle and yelled, "*¡Vente carnero!*" Then you rushed for the fence.

Sometimes out of nowhere Emilio Sánchez appeared on his bowlegged and bony horse, rope in hand, ready for the first kid he could capture as we all ran for the front door of the school. Except for Lorenzo, a low-slung kid with hands that hung to his knees, Emilio almost never roped any of us. When he did lasso the *chango* kid, Emilio would drag his catch along the weeds up to the door of the school and yell to the teacher, "Ees dis won of jours?"

She was the only *gringa* most of us had ever known up close. Mrs. Majors, our teacher, was big, mean, and red-faced, with a car-horn voice that would start at the front of the schoolroom where the first graders sat and thunderclap to the back where José Torres, the only sixth grader, was king.

There was gossip in our village about Mrs. Majors. They said she had studied to be in the movies, or maybe just opera. I had never seen a movie, and I thought opera was like having your appendix taken out. They said something had ruined her chords so she couldn't sing anymore—maybe a very bad sore throat that had only left her a thunder voice. The story changed a little every time I heard it. Some said she was even a virgin, but I doubted it. How could Mrs. Majors be like *La Virgen?* Anyway, she had left the big city for a faraway place to hide forever. Maybe she was pointed to Capulín by some evil spirit who wanted to punish us children; her old Ford ended up stuck in the *caliche,* the clay of the *cuesta del puerto,* after one of our not so regular thunderstorms.

The U.S. Forest Service didn't like sagebrush and that is how *El Grande,* my grandmother from my mother's side, found Mrs. Majors. With their big yellow machines the *floresta* had plowed the *chamisal* under and instead planted a new kind of buffalo grass. After years the range was finally green and ready for grazing by cows with permits, like El Grande's herd of eighty, the most of anybody in the valley. El Grande was good to the *floresta.* He put out forest fires, so the ranger liked him and gave him first crack. El Grande was proud of being the U.S. Forest's pet; all day he had roamed the range on his horse checking it out, no matter the rain.

As he rode he came to a giant woman sitting on a stump on the side of the road crying, her car in the ditch. El Grande's horse bolted, as they do when they spot a bear in the brush or maybe a snake. Finally calm, they moved closer to see her. Had he come face to face with *La Llorona,* the spirit woman who stalks the night crying? When she saw him she screamed with joy and hobbled toward the horse, splattering mud. The horse reared. El Grande yelled to her to stop, but the woman didn't know Spanish so she kept coming. The horse backed away. Not knowing what else to do, El Grande pulled out his rope and lassoed the woman around what might be her waist. The horse, a roper, tightened and sidestepped toward the nearest *piñón* tree. Two quick trips around the tree, a fast hitch on a low branch, and the strange muddy woman was under control.

Pedro Valdez had been to the state hospital to pick up his nephew, Malvino. The muddy Chevy pickup slid to a stop at the bottom of *la cuesta* where *caliche* was king, and after a rain everybody knew to stop and put on chains. From the side of the hill El Grande came and slid to a stop, too. He told them of the English-speaking woman he had tied to a tree. Malvino was crazy but he knew English so they all went to see, with Malvino in front to make sure it was safe. Strange to find a woman, much less a *gringa*, all alone in the *ex-chamisal*. But they had to help her, so they loaded all of her onto the truck. No need for chains now. With that much weight not even a Chevy needed chains for the sticky *caliche*.

Capulín had no hotel, no police, and no place to put an English-speaking stranger, so Pedro was stuck with a ton of woman he couldn't talk to—to say nothing about the attention she might bring. *Señora* Valdez would not find peace when Pedro showed up with a woman in the back of his truck. But Pedro was smart. He arrived at the front of his barn with Malvino and his "private *consejera*" from the state hospital. Her job was to keep Malvino sane.

There were no secrets in Capulín. The story of what had happened at *la cuesta* spread like prairie fire and grew larger as it went. For the next few days people found many excuses for visiting Pedro and trying to sneak a peek into his barn. Malvino thought he was the famous one; who would want to miss out on all the attention? He stayed sane and everything worked.

Río Arriba was the county seat and from there, fatefully, came word that the teacher assigned to us refused to come. "No light, no running water, no inside toilet, no teacher," she had said. The village mothers panicked. We children were in a heaven full of joy. No teacher, no school, no homework—just dodging rams. The county said it would take time to find a new one, so find a substitute, or delay opening school. Wait, I prayed.

As luck would have it my father was one of them: a teacher. But his school was in the next village downstream, Coyote. He was not allowed to teach in his own village as punishment for being a Republican in a county that was Democrat. So snow, rain, or sunshine—off to Coyote he went everyday. He, El Grande, and a few other men went to Pedro's barn and no doubt promised Mrs. Majors the earth and the moon if she said yes. They said she wasn't qualified, but she spoke English well enough.

Mrs. Majors and I did not see eye to eye from the first day of school. For one thing, she couldn't take a joke. The bright new bell they had put on a cement altar in front of the school that summer was more sacred than the *camposanto,* graveyard, of the Jicarillas. But nobody told me. On the first day I walked quickly on the trail along the edge of the deep arroyo and up the *mesita* to school. Maybe it was because I had spent all summer listening to my brother Juan's wild stories that I couldn't control it. I climbed the altar. TAWAAANG, TAWAAANG, TAWAAANG!

"STOP! Stop ringing that damn bell!" Her thunder voice bit my ears like a giant fly.

"AW GO TO HELL!" Instinct, no doubt. The words came out *automáticamente.* I remember moving through the air like a spear aimed at the door of the school. Then came the desks; I hit somewhere around the end of the third grade. Books flew and the stars twinkled bright against a black sky, but thank God only for a second, maybe two. I rose into the air again, now the other way out the door. But this time the ground came up slowly, just about where the trail back home started.

"Don't come back," I heard her call through the fog in a bitter voice.

As I walked along, still a little punchy, toward the deep arroyo, some scary thoughts began to come together in my mind. School was going to be very different. Mrs. Majors was a different kind of teacher, for sure. Were all *gringos* this mean? Or was I a bad person? Who would ever guess I could get into so much trouble the first day of school?

Our house was a low-hanging, long adobe place with a room added to it every time my parents had a new kid. The Capulín Cash Store was finally added at the end. We sold everything from nails to St. Joseph aspirins. My mother ran it. Across the dirt road El Grande had his castle, with an attic even. On the back side, where the sun didn't shine all day, was the smokehouse where all the meat was kept and where the fine leather *reata,* the dreaded fine-leather whip, hung from a nail. El Grande used it to enforce the law around the family. And sometimes even the village. When somebody was born, they came to notify him. When somebody was very sick, they came to notify him. When the sick or old finally died, he was called to make sure there was no foul play. They called him *Don* Ezequiel and he was always in charge.

I slunk around the corner of the house full of pains, glad to remember that my father had left early for Coyote. He would, of course, see Mrs. Majors' side of the story. I walked into the front of the store looking, no doubt, like a sick little customer.

"¿Por qué no 'stás en la escuela?" My mother asked as she looked up from where she knelt to stack cans of oil. "What happened?"

I tried to talk but the words couldn't get past the lump. "I... I did something evil. To the new teacher. She threw me out of school and now I'll have to be dumb forever." With that, I started to cry. Who would want to be stupid all day and all night?

"What did you do?"

"I rang the new bell." She stared at me with the look that told me I'd be an orphan if I didn't tell the truth.

"AND?" Every letter got bigger.

"And when the teacher yelled to quit I... I said something Juan says all the time."

"What?"

"I told her to go where the devil lives."

"To hell, Flavio?"

"Yes," I said like the little mouse in the comics.

"¡Ave María Purísima!" she prayed as she raised her eyes to heaven.

I waited for God to open the sky and hit me with something. But for a long while nothing happened.

"Since your father isn't here, you must go across the road and tell your *Papá Grande* what you did... *Vaya.*"

Then I realized what God was going to get me with... the leather *reata* that hung in the smokehouse. "Please, please... pleeze!" I begged as I went to my knees. "I don't even know how to say the awful words in Spanish."

For a long time she thought about the whole thing. She even looked out the window across the road.

"Okay, *chamaco sinvergüenza.* Just this one time. But for the rest of the day you will chop enough firewood to last until I don't even know when. Maybe Christmas."

Who said prayers don't get answered? With the double *filo* ax I pounded away at the woodpile all morning and all afternoon. Wheelbarrow after wheelbarrow full of pine, cedar, and even oak *leños* paraded to the porch of the store where I stacked the firewood neatly. I even forgot lunch. By the time the sun was resting on top of the school and turning red, I had cut enough wood to keep the potbelly in the middle of the store hot for the winter.

By the middle of the next day my mother had put me back in school, but I could tell that Mrs. Majors wasn't finished with the whole thing.

I volunteered to clean the blackboard and even raised my hand to answer. She didn't ask. When ram time came I stayed back, just in case Mrs. Majors needed something. She didn't ask. I finally asked if I could light the potbelly for her. She said it was still summer. She added, "stupid."

After that, I vowed to get very smart. I would learn all about the R.E.A. and the new saw mill that people in the village were talking about, and I would even listen closely to everything Mr. Beatty had to say on the radio. I would show the *vieja* from who knows where. I would show Mrs. Majors good.

In my mother's store, where the men came to talk more than to buy, I began my education. Around the potbelly they sat to exchange *chismes*. First the R.E.A. They said the *gobierno* was going to bring electricity to the valley. Some said the wires would hiss all night and scare the game away. Some said the wires would shine so the animals would get no sleep. And others said the grasshoppers would have a clear shot at the crops day and night. "Who knows?" some said.

But the R.E.A. people were going to show them. Word spread that they were going to bring a movie for the people of the village to see the miracle of electricity. I had never seen a movie but had heard about them from my oldest sister, Dolores, who had been to the movies in Santa Fe. I wasn't sure about electricity, but I was sure I wanted to see the movie. I prayed to God that nothing would happen to the R.E.A., like getting stuck at *la cuesta*.

They also talked about the *Duque Ceety* (lumber company) and how it was going to build a sawmill just beyond Emilio's land to make boards for houses in the city. They talked about roads into the deep forest for trucks to haul logs. Shooting deer in the summer would be risky. City slicker *pendejos* who have no respect would come, maybe even more *gringos* like Mrs. Majors.

The *platicas* around the potbelly started most of the time in the late afternoon, when the men were finished with their work. Each man would come in the door, push his hat back a little bit and say, *"¿Cómo estamos, muchachos?"* He would then walk over to the stove to see if it was hot, even in the summer. He would then scratch his privates a little and sit down on an old chair or stack of firewood. All the others there would give him a glance, take a slow drag from their Bull Durham roll-your-own and continue talking. They were all cousins, brothers, uncles, or just *compadres*.

Ahh! But when El Grande came in everybody put out his smoke, stood up, and said, *"Buenas tardes,* Don Ezequiel." Somebody would get him a chair and he would always refuse it before he sat down. It was polite. El Grande always talked last, and everybody always listened. He told the men the government would do to us what it had done to the Indians, the Jicarilla and the Navajo.

It would make promises but not keep them.

He told them of the troubles that were coming, and they knew he was right. He always was.

DOS

Homework, housework, ranchowork. This time of year everybody worked. The last cut of the alfalfa was ready, the chokecherries were purple, the *chiles* on the vine were getting red, and at school we were already to fractions. Who would think a fourth and a fourth equals a half was so important? Potatoes, too; everybody came to help El Grande *cosechar papas* by the hundreds of hundred-pound sacks. The chokecherries were turned into jam or syrup and the *chiles* were strung up into *ristras* and hung on the sunny side of the house, looking like blood dripping from the roof. Mrs. Majors was putting on more weight, getting ready for winter, no doubt. And at school we were always looking for the common denominator, figuring out what a fourth and a third was all together.

Soon all the cows would be rounded up and brought home. The calves were sold to the *gringos* who came in big trucks, and for weeks the mother cows cried all night so we couldn't sleep. How sad to sell your kids, I thought, even if they are as ugly as the *chango* kid Lorenzo. "Flavio, even the gorilla thinks her babies are cute," my father always said.

We had pigs, too, and Sundays were pig-rodeo time. Early in the morning the pigs would start digging up leftovers from one end of the potato patch to the other. By close to noon they had all the potatoes they could swallow and headed across the valley to the mud baths at the lower end of the *vega*. There were maybe ten big pigs and countless little piggies. But the queen of the herd was a huge, mean gray sow. She ate, slept, and took her mud bath wherever she wanted; and nobody asked questions. We called her *La Aprovechada,* because she liked to bully the other pigs. If you were crazy enough to ride her, you were the bravest in the world, and only my sister Cordelia had tried. We called her Sergeant Cordy.

When El Grande and La Grande left for church, we sneaked out to the willow thicket at the edge of the *vega* and climbed one of the big willow trees to get a good look at the wallowing pigs. Upon the signal from Cordy, we would creep quietly through the tall grass until the first pig made a noise, like he knew we were there. We waited. The pigs settled back down.

"CHARGE!" Cordy yelled, and each of us would head for a muddy pig, pounce on its back and away we went, always toward the willow thicket. Pigs don't buck and kick. They dance and bite. If they can't lose you with fancy steps, they run under a low branch. We had to ride way up front, almost on their necks, or they would turn around and eat our legs, shoes and all. High on the hog! The ride was short, but so much fun our memories of the leather *reata* hanging in the smokehouse got lost in the mud.

Then there was *La Aprovechada.* She didn't like anybody making a rodeo out of her family. As soon as we hit the ground, we had to bounce up a tree because a mountain of pig was likely to be headed for us, looking for something to chew.

This one Sunday started like all the others, peaceful and quiet, church bells full of God. Cordy, Juan, and I crawled along the *vega* floor like brown snakes looking for a meal. In a flash the snakes turned into *vaqueros* and away we went, mud flying and pigs grunting towards the willow thicket. Sure enough, right behind us *La Aprovechada* was having one of her days. Lucky for us she was so big; it made her slow. Juan jumped off his pig and ran for a tree. Cordy fell and ran for the same tree while I was catching a low-hanging branch on the chest.

"Run, *pendéjo!*" they yelled from up high. I got to the tree about a second before the ton of pork. Lucky for me they reached down and pulled me up—one by the suspenders of my Levi's overalls and the other by my hair. Safe.

Flashing her big yellow teeth and circling the tree, *La Aprovechada* was no doubt mad because she lost again. All the other times she had been a good sport. She would go back to the mud baths with the other pigs so we could climb down, sneak home, the rodeo over for another Sunday. But this time she lay down and went to sleep. Under our tree. We looked down, then at each other. Then down again. We waited for a little while more. Cordy started humming about a "home on the range" while we swayed slowly back and forth with the afternoon breeze. Juan broke a long twig and poked the pig with it. She grunted twice, but didn't move.

"Oye, Aprovechada desgraciada, vete al soquete," I yelled my part.

Cordy reached over and kicked me. "Shaddup. You're going to cause somebody to find us and then El Grande will come. Do you want to die of *reatazos* or what?"

The breeze kicked up and the skinny willow tree gave little cracking sounds; but there we were, afraid to stay, afraid to go. As the afternoon moved along, I began to think this was not my favorite way to spend the Lord's Day. Maybe even church was better. Juan seemed to be asleep, and Cordy was thinking about whatever girls think.

Honk—Hooonk! It was the horn of my father's truck. My mother used it to signal that dinner was ready. If you didn't get there fast, you didn't eat. If you didn't get there at all, you'd better start looking for another family.

"Juan, are you awake?" Cordy whispered up the tree.

"Yeah, but if you think I'm going to run for it you are crazy. Better up a tree than down a pig," he said.

"All right. I'll do it myself," she said, disgusted. "If the pig eats me, don't tell them where I went. Mother will worry." She slid slowly and quietly down the tree, with one eye across the open space to the wooden gate that led into the vega and the other on sleeping beauty under the tree. When she got down to the last branch she stopped and listened to the pig breathe. Then very quietly she put one foot on the ground between the pig's feet, and listened some more. Then the other foot. Still no noise. She bolted for the wooden gate, her two black braids flying behind her. *La Aprovechada* rolled to her feet, took two steps, and figured it was no use. She turned and went back to sleep. "Hey, *changos* in the trees. Who's next?" Cordy yelled proudly.

"Every man for his self," Juan said as he worked his way down the tree. I started to cry. "You wake her up and I knock you off the tree," he scolded. Through foggy tears I saw him reach the ground and tiptoe to the fence. The pig didn't move.

I had not been so scared since my trouble with Mrs. Majors. But if they could do it, I had to do it. I slid down from branch to branch until I was close to the ground. The pig looked asleep and I slowly put both feet down to the ground. Still hanging on to the last branch, I looked over to check the pig.

Her eyes were open and her blonde eyelashes were pointing straight at me.

GRUUUNT! Two creatures, one human and one pork, streaked across the patch of meadow toward the fence where Cordy and Juan were cheering for one of us. The pig was gaining on me. My short, sinful life flashed in front of me. It had been good, but it would soon be over. I saw Cordy jump off the gate with El Grande's *garrote,* his thick stick which he kept by the gate to defend himself from the very pig that was about to eat me. Cordy took up a batter's stance like the Babe Ruth we had always heard about on the radio. She started her swing about the time I was even with her, and in the next instant I heard a "Craaack" from someplace behind me. Then, "Grunt, grunt." I reached the gate and Juan flipped me over the top and down to the dust on the other side. Up on one knee, I saw Cordy flying over the gate and a pig on rubber legs looking for the right way to the mud.

Laughing with our arms around each other's necks, we headed out of the *vega* and up the hill toward the house. When we got near the top, we saw him. El Grande had been sitting near the outhouse, no doubt watching the show down in the *vega*.

First came the *reata*. Then no dinner. I stayed awake most of the night holding a wet rag to my back part and thinking about the ups and downs of life.

TRES

Coyotes eat sheep and that is how I ended up a mother. In a stormy night that spring they came in a pack, sneaked into the corral and killed a sheep but left the lamb. In the morning El Grande found the mess, blood and guts all over, and the baby just shivering there, hungry and scared. In the *emergencia* of the day I was called into action to feed the little wooly thing with a Coke bottle full of cow's milk through a rubber nipple. At first he didn't know how to suck it. He would get so excited he would snap the nipple off and the milk would pour all over him. I would get mad and make him drink, nipple or not. After a while the little sheep and I had what you might call an understanding. We quit pretending I was a sheep with rubber chi-chies from the Coca-Cola store, and just went for the bottle.

From work it went to love, not only because I was sorry for him but because none of the other sheep liked him. Whenever he got close to any of them they always had a little hate to hand out. So instead of going off to the upper *vega* with the sheep, he got to hanging around the house. After awhile his friends became the dogs, Chulo, Pope, and Laddie. The *perros* liked him because they could lick his face after every meal and get a little milk snack. By the time we celebrated the independence of America that summer, there were four lazy bums sleeping in the tall weeds below the porch of the Capulín Cash Store—three dogs and a sheep. So when it came time to give him a name, what else could I do? I named him Perro.

When Perro and the dogs needed a little fun in the cool afternoon they would lie around on the side of the road and wait for cars to chase. There weren't many cars on the dirt road through Capulín, but when one finally came the dogs would run and bark at the tires halfway to the bridge over the Rio Capulín. The lamb would run along behind them, no doubt trying to figure out the name of the game. When the dogs got tired they came back to the tall weeds and Perro would climb onto the porch to lick the empty bottles stacked in cases in one corner. He never licked the Nehi or the Seven-up, just the Cokes.

Perro became almost as famous as Mrs. Majors. People who came to the store always asked about him. Little kids would pat him on the head like a dog, and he would wag his tail. Some even got him a Coke bottle to lick. And the dogs gave him fleas.

This particular Saturday in November was no regular Saturday. It was warm, cloudless, and about to explode. I got up, patted my face with a little cold water to get the spice of life flowing and headed across the dirt road to have breakfast with El Grande as I did almost every Saturday. I loved my Mama Grande's breakfasts because she had a special way of cooking. She was from the Jacques family, the people with the light-green eyes and the very black hair. My mother always said there was a little French in everything she cooked. It was always the same: A stack of fresh tortillas, *chorizo con huevos*, red *chile* with dried deer meat and *papitas*. And on top of everything, a little lemony thing with cheese in it. Plus a little pitcher of chokecherry syrup to finish off the tortillas. For herself, coffee. El Grande never drank coffee because he said it would rot your insides. But he sure ate a lot of everything else.

"What are we going to do today?" I asked him after the last burp, sure that he would have some smart thing to say. He was quiet, as though his mind were far away. "Are you sick? How about let's walk up the hill to the you-know-what?" He didn't answer. After a long while and many looks out the kitchen window, he stood up and put on his same old sweaty hat.

"Vente conmigo, hijo," he said all official. Out the door and over to the shed where he had his saddles, harnesses, and ropes. He took a rope from a hook on the wall and turned to look me straight in the eye. "Flavio, today is a fine day. Today is the day we must butcher your Perro."

"NO!" I cried. "What are you saying? We can't kill my Perro! He's mine! He doesn't know he's a sheep. I'm his mother almost!"

"The time has come when you must let him go. *Como los hombres. La muerte es parte de la vida."* Then, as if he didn't even care, he added that Mama Grande needed the meat for the kitchen.

"I hate you. Why don't you kill one of those other ones? Maybe one of those damn goats that is always going off to the alfalfa and causing trouble," I begged.

"Watch your language," he ordered.

"He won't even taste right, he thinks he's a dog. He's always chasing cars and licking bottles. Who wants to eat dog?"

"Let me explain something to you, *hijo*. Part of being a man is that sometimes you must do things that hurt your *muchisimo*. You must recognize that you cannot always do what is easy. You must learn to deal with the joy of life and the pain of death with the same dignity. It is better to pain a little now than to suffer a lot later." He put his big, rough hand on my shoulder. Tears rolled down my face as I pictured my Perro dead. "You see, Perro is not like the rest of them. He does not graze like the rest of the flock. He does not have the same fears. He does not know to huddle to stay warm in winter. He has never learned what the dangers are. When winter comes he will freeze to death or the coyotes will kill him. It is better if we do it now."

For a long time we didn't say anything. I knew he was always right, but I didn't want to believe it. Part of me thought that maybe this time he was wrong. Finally he stood up. I knew that the time for thinking was over.

"Ok. But I'm not going to help you today. I'm going home," I said.

"No! You must take part. Face it even if it hurts. If you don't it will be worse. If you help you will soon know it was the right thing to do. If you don't you will always wonder. *Vamos.*" He handed me the rope as he started up the little hill to the corral.

I thought of throwing the rope at him and running home to hide under the bed. Someday I would disobey him and it might as well be now. I thought for a little more, blew my nose, and rubbed my eyes. I followed him up the hill.

The sheep were up and ready for feeding while the goats had already jumped the fence and wandered to the slope for grazing. When we came into the corral, all the sheep ran to the other end, but Perro came over, tail wagging, thinking we were there for a friendly visit. I stopped for a moment and looked at El Grande, but his face was made of stone. I petted Perro's head and slipped the rope over his neck. He no doubt thought we were on our way to enjoy a little Coca Cola on the porch of the Capulín Cash Store. Instead I led him down the hill toward the big cedar tree next to the storage shed.

All my life I had watched sheep, goats, calves, and even pigs get hanged from a hind leg and have the blood of life gush from their throats into a bent pan with a quick slit from El Grande's long knife with the deerhorn handle. Before you could even get used to the smell of death, he would have the hide off and would be ready to open the animal. Out came intestines, stomach and a whole bunch of other pink, gray, red, and purple things. Some you could eat and some not. I always asked how he knew which were the ones you could cook and eat. He always answered, "If you eat one and you die you know it isn't any good to eat."

Today I wasn't in the mood for questions. I tried to think of all the problems Perro had given me, like having to feed him, clean up after him, even looking for him when he got lost. I still felt sick, like throwing up.

"Give me your leg, *Perrito,*" I heard him say. I flung the rope I was holding and ran toward the vega, past the pig wallows and up on top of a haystack at the edge of the *encinal*. I fell on the hay, barely able to catch my breath. I knew I was in trouble. El Grande would think I was a coward. Right then I didn't care. I just lay there looking at the clear blue sky thinking about all the places I would like to visit, like the moon, Japan, maybe even Santa Fe. I thought of Mrs. Majors and how she could be a virgin, old as she was. And I even sneaked a little thought about what might be going on back at the hanging tree. Why hadn't God helped out this time? I wondered. I got very sleepy.

The animals of the deep forest came with much fear and excitement to where I stood. The deer, bear, coyote, rabbit, and even the birds. From all directions they came with the same cry. "The *abuelo* is coming! The *abuelo* is coming!" What did they mean? At Christmas the abuelo is the mean, masked boogeyman that beats your butt around the *luminarias* for not behaving. But *abuelo* also means grandfather. Whichever it was, the animals begged me to help them figure out what to do. The beaver wanted to build a deep pond so that we could all hide under water. The deer begged everybody to run away. And the groundhog wanted to hide in a deep hole in the ground. As they all tried to talk first we suddenly saw a black, shaggy monster with horns and a pointed tail running through the forest setting fires with a torch. Smoke made the sky dark. More animals ran from the forest. I could feel the heat on my face. "What shall we do?" they all asked. "We will stand our ground. Put the fires out with water from the *río.* We must show the *abuelo* we are not afraid!" All the animals cheered at my grand plan.

"¡CARAMBA, MUCHACHO!" His voice boomed in my ears like the school bell. I came up spring-loaded off the hay. His huge chocolate face with the big Pancho Villa mustache was right next to mine. It was all out of shape with laughter. When I was more awake I saw that his sleeves were rolled up to his elbows and his shirt and pants were splattered with blood. *"Hijo, siéntate aquí,"* he said as he pointed to a spot next to the fence. He sat back against the haystack and crossed his arms in front of his big belly. First he said he was not mad at me. He understood what Perro meant to me. Then he said that every man must know the difference between the easy way out and how much he can take. He said he was proud of me for taking Perro to the hanging tree. For a little while he said nothing more. Finally he leaned toward me and whispered that it had bothered him, too.

We walked back across the *vega,* each one with his own thoughts. In a day or two Mama Grande's red *chile* would have fresh meat in it and I would think it tasted just fine.

CUATRO

Perro was dead and gone to wherever orphans go. The deer season was over, but no matter because El Grande only hunted before and sometimes after. And some said that Mrs. Majors was sneaking little visits to Emilio's tool shed for who knows what. Of most *importancia* was that the day for the movie about the R.E.A. and electricity had, by the mercy of God, finally come. Signs announcing it had come in the mail, and my mother posted them in the store and on the gas pump. She was supposed to decide where the movie would be, the school or the church. Some said not the church. It would discredit the saints. If God heard there was a movie in there He would send his own electricity in a thunderbolt, my Tío Rosendo had said. Mrs. Majors said that it was education, so in the school it should go. She told us that if we didn't do our homework she wouldn't let us in the door. When she stood square in the door, not even the moscas could sneak past. I guess my mother agreed, and since there were no saints to discredit in our school, the school was it. For those few days before the movie you would have thought that every kid in Capulín was a pure scholar.

Long before the movie, the R.E.A. was already working on where the power line would go. *Los hombres eléctricos,* as some called them, had been cutting trees and marking the way with little stakes tied with bright red ribbons. Other men had gone to people's houses asking for *permiso* to put poles on their land. At first, most, said no. When the men came back waving papers and saying they would bring the court, people got scared and signed. And this is how the war of the red ribbons started.

La guerra de los listones was fought at night. When the *hombres eléctricos* were gone, I and some of the guys from school—Leo, Watchate, Ricardo, and sometimes even the ape kid—wormed our way into the *vegas*, the pastures, the cornfields, and even the deep forest, to pull up the stakes and stick them in other places. We all took a red ribbon and wrapped it around our arm to show that we were soldiers in the war against electricity. If you were a man without a red ribbon, you were a man with no *huevos.*

At first the enemy would come in the morning and do the work all over again, move the little stakes back to where they were supposed to be. But at night we came and moved them again.

Then they got bigger and longer ones and stuck them deeper. At night we came and cut them with the ax. Finally they quit fixing things and we thought we had won. But one day huge trucks, some with giant drills, and others loaded with logs longer than any that grew in the deep forest, rolled up in front of the store. I spotted them on my way home from school, hit the dirt behind the wood pile, and took off my ribbon. I felt my *huevos* shrinking away. But in war you do what you gotta do to keep from getting captured. I sneaked up to the back door of the store, which was unlocked, and tiptoed into the storeroom. My mother, not a soldier herself, was asking them questions. All her life she had been good at asking questions. It was a little hard to hear the answers, but enough came through: poles, powerline, before winter, and light up like a city. They were laughing. I could smell the cigarettes they were smoking and knew we had lost the war. Our ax was no match for their huge logs.

I sat down on a big sack of beans. From a stack of cartons nearby, I pulled a box of oatmeal, the round box with a white-haired, smiling American in the picture. I pulled the string to open it and ate it raw. What else could I do? Sometimes when you think you've lost everything, all you can do is eat.

But after a few hard swallows I ran over to the edge of the deep arroyo and yelled the well-known "Come quick." The guys came running and I told them the bad news. Not ready to taste defeat, they said, "Show us." We ran to the lower side of the porch where the nesting weeds of Perro and the dogs were now brown. We peeked around the corner. There they still were. New, shiny trucks that said Dodge in front and Power Wagon on the side; and below, 4-Wheel Drive. We didn't know what that was; Capulín's cars just barely had wheels. They were loaded with all kinds of things we had never even seen before and sat waiting for the drivers who no doubt knew where to stick the poles. We all looked at one another, sweating heavily. Then we sat back in the weeds and passed around the oatmeal. When dark finally hit the Capulín valley, we all went home, another army worse off than Mr. Beatty's red Chinamen.

The late, cold afternoon of movie day had finally dragged by, and the regulars gathered around the potbelly in the store. Each one came in saying, *"Hijo 'e la patada, cómo 'stá frío,"* scratching his crotch and reaching for his little sack of Bull Durham in his shirt pocket. Some could roll one with one hand! Nobody smoked readyrolls. My job was to keep the stove going, which I didn't mind because I could stick around and listen to all the *chismes* of the community. The men talked about the powerline, the dust in the air and the weather; but it seemed that nobody wanted to talk about the movie. It was as if *machos* didn't talk about those things.

Finally I couldn't stand it any longer. "Is everybody going to the movie tonight?" I asked. Nobody answered. Maybe nobody dared. El Grande finally wondered out loud where it was going to be, as if he didn't know.

Three brave ones said, *"La escuela."* Then another one asked what it was all about, as if he didn't know.

"Electricity," I said. They all glared at me. But before I knew it, everybody was talking and laughing again.

"With good light, my wife's cooking is going to get better," Pedro said. They laughed.

"I am going to put a light in my hen house to keep my rooster happy," said another.

"I am going to have enough light to read a letter I got from the U.S. Army seven years ago; I think it's my discharge," said Roberto; and they all laughed.

"I want a light in my outhouse so I can see the pictures in the Sears catalog," El Grande said. Now they really laughed.

"I better hustle home and get my wife to the movie," said the bravest one. They all scooted out of the store in a big hurry.

I followed El Grande across the road to his house so he could get dressed up; which just meant that he traded his old, torn up hat for his new hat. He also had to get official. Whenever anything important happened in the village, he was in charge—and to show it he always carried his 30-30 hex-barrel Winchester cradled across his arms. When he had his gun with him, he was *Don* Ezequiel.

We walked together across the deep arroyo and up the *mesita* toward the school. It was still a little early, but, already anxious, people had picked their seats in the front rows. *Tío* Casimiro was there. He was very old, nearly blind, almost deaf, and knew no English. When El Grande spoke to him he gave us a toothless smile and said he was ready for the movie. The movie people were running around checking wires and trying to start their gasoline generator. More and more people came in and before long it was the biggest crowd since the funeral of Chucho Montes, who was the first one to have ever worked for the U.S. Forest as a deputy ranger. The only reason people came to his funeral was to make sure he was really dead.

A hush suddenly hit the crowd as the generator started outside the window. A tall *gringo* stepped up to the front of the room and smiled at everybody. He had clean white teeth and no hair. Everybody clapped.

"Good evening, ladies and gentlemen. On behalf of the Rural Electrification Administration, I would like to welcome all of you here tonight. I know that many of you don't understand English, and I am sorry to say I don't *habla español!*" He gave a squeaky, nervous laugh. The people clapped a little. "Perhaps it doesn't really matter, since the wonderful film you are about to see tells it all in pictures."

I wished he would shut up and get the movie going.

"You are about to see the miracle of electricity through the eyes of a farm family much like many of the families right here in Cape-u-line. Ahhm. Before we begin I have been asked to remind you that much equipment such as wire, insulators, and braces will soon be distributed all along the route of the powerline. All that equipment, including the little wooden stakes with the pretty red ribbons, is government property and destroying any of it is a crime."

I took a quick look around the room and caught Leo's eye, and on the other side, Watchate's. We had given him that name because he was always scared of everything and kept saying, "Watch out." Right now Watchate might be right. I wanted to stand up and say I give up, but lucky for me the *gringo* went on.

"I am sure that no one here wants to delay the progress of electrification." Everybody looked around to see who had blood on his hands, or maybe just shifty eyes. I thought everybody was looking at me.

"¿Qué dice ese pela'o?" Tío Casimiro leaned over and asked me, right in the middle of the tension.

"He said we better not rob their stakes," I explained.

"Pues, ¿qué piensa, que semos ladrones, ese hijo de la chingada?" he blasted in a booming voice. The room exploded with laughter. Some held their bellies and others slapped their knees. Still others shook their heads, not believing what the old man had said. Chingada was a word you didn't use in polite company. I didn't dare translate for the *gringo.*

Finally the noise in the room died down and the *gringo,* still as little confused about what had happened, spoke again.

"Would anyone have any question whatsoever, please?" Nobody moved. "Well, then, without any further delay, let us proceed with the wonderful world of electricity."

The lanterns were turned off and some backwards numbers flashed on the screen. My heart pounded. The music started and there it was, a sunflower moving across a cornfield. Suddenly, the cornfield ended and you could see it was a kid carrying the sunflower on a long stalk. When the kid got home, electricity had come and his mother was showing off her new electric things. And from there things got better. Electric everything! Even an electric machine to milk the cows. It was ugly. Our cows would never stand for that. I glanced at El Grande, who had a big smile. *Tío* Casimiro had a smile, and a spit string hanging down to his lap. The *gringo* had said it would last an hour, but it was over before I knew it. As "The End" flashed on the screen, the *gringo* lit two light bulbs in front of the room. Everybody was blinded and everybody clapped. Somebody in the back yelled, *"¡Orale¡"* Everybody clapped again.

"That's electricity, folks!" the *gringo* said with a big smile.

People rubbed their eyes and squinted in the bright room. Nobody was complaining about electricity now. The R.E.A. had blown up the last of the *renegados,* no question.

Everybody was smiling and talking happily, except El Grande. He had the look he wore the morning he told me it was time for my Perro to go. *"Silencio... Silencio, por favor,"* he said as he stood up in the middle of the room with his rifle in his arms like a baby.

The chatter died and everybody looked at him. They all knew that he had something important to say. They listened *con respeto.*

"I want to say what I have been thinking. Some might not agree, and that is your right. But I must say this. I came to this valley many, many years ago as a boy. Now I am an old man. I have seen many things come and go. Winter and summer. Rain and drought. Health and sickness. Birth and death. I have seen these mountains give with kindness and take with anger. We the people have always understood it is God's will. Now I am worried. The Indian in me speaks. He says we are losing our respect for the land, the wind, the sky. The only electricity we have ever known has come from the clouds. Now it will come from the wires. The Christian in me speaks, too. He says we are losing our respect for each other. Electricity, the *molino,* the roads into the forest, the machines, the new people that will come. We are losing what our forefathers taught us. Our children will not have the same peace we have known. Already there are rumors that the government made the *atómica* that was thrown at the Japanese right over the mountain in *la sierra de los alamos.* All of you know what la bomba atómica did. We could not stop the *atómica,* and I do not think we can stop all this. Each one of you must deal with it in your own way. That is all I have to say."

The men in the back of the room, who had been passing the pint of Hill & Hill, stood very still. Kids sat quietly. The *gringo* with the light bulbs just stood and smiled.

An old woman with a brown fur coat that made her look like a bear stood up. "Don Ezequiel *dice bien.* He is a very wise man and we have always followed everything he said."

Everybody clapped, as if to agree with the her.

El Grande sat there as if he didn't like what he heard.

"Pero con muchísimo respeto, I want to say something more," the woman started again. "The electricos have stolen

our hearts. My little *adobe casita* out by the arroyo has two little windows and a big crack under the door. In the winter I sit there next to the *estufa* trying to keep warm with no light, to save the oil in my *lampara*. I ask you, how long can you sit in the dark, freezing, wondering what the *cucarachas* are doing to your house?"

The people looked around slowly, as if their necks almost didn't work, eyes like little slits. Do the *cucarachas* even walk around the house in the winter, I wondered.

"*¡Vieja llorona!*" *Tío* Casimiro finally yelled from right next to me. "It is better if you stay in the dark because that way you don't scare the little kids when they are coming from school. The *eléctricos* have chopped off your head, *pendeja.*" He pointed more or less to where the *gringo* with the bulbs was still standing. The *gringo* shifted from foot to foot and the people all laughed.

"*¡Viejo ciego... que sabes tú!* If you are blind, what do you care if there is electric lights or not? But for me, I want to see my little *casita* at night. And some day maybe even get me an iron or one of those teevees they talk about. *Progreso.* That's what we need in Capulín." She sat down.

About this time the *gringo* came over and grabbed me by the arm and asked me what was happening. I guess he figured if I could tell *Tío* Casimiro what was said, I could tell him, too. I told him they were saying that he had cut off the bear woman's head, more or less. He looked at me weirdly. His mouth fell open and the rest of his face wrinkled.

"Hold it, folks! I am very sorry if any of you have misunderstood. We are just interested in Cape-u-line becoming electrified, just as the government wants you to. No heads will be cut off here. Please."

"We don't want your electric lights, *vato,*" one of the Hill & Hill guys yelled from the back.

"You chaddup your mouth, *borracho,*" one of the other women yelled from the corner. "What do you know? All of the women here are the ones that have to cook in the dark for you *huevones* who won't even go get wood no more. We want the lights and be like those *gringos* in the movie. Don Ezequiel is always right, but he is a man, too." All the women clapped and laughed and the men glanced around as if they were looking for somebody to punch with a big *chingaso*.

But nobody said more. One at a time the people started out the door. After almost everybody was out, El Grande walked slowly, hat in his hand, to the same door.

CINCO

"Hey, where's the electric heater that was in the movie the other *noche?* I sure could use it *ahora,*" I thought out loud as I walked across the road to check up on El Grande. It was a cold morning and already the tops of the San Juans to the *norte* were white. Winter has a way of sneaking up on you before your bones are even ready, I thought.

I opened the door to the *sala* and got hit in the nose with the smell of baking bread. El Grande's little *vieja,* as he called my *abuelita*, was up to her Saturday morning goodies. He had built a big fire in the adobe fireplace and was now asleep, snoring like the summer frogs of the *vega.* I walked into the kitchen to say my *buenos días,* sneaked a brown beauty still hot from the oven, and went back into the *sala* to wait for the frogs to finish the song. As I lay there on the sheepskin near the fire, I noticed that the man and woman in the egg-shaped picture with the curved glass were looking right at me. If I moved to one side, their eyes followed me. I stood on a chair and they looked up. The picture had been there forever, but they had never looked at me like that. Do all pictures do that? Does it have to do with the curved glass in front? Who are those two, anyway? I'm glad it's not night, I finally told myself.

"*¡Quizás me dormí!*" he said as his eyes snapped open. He must have fallen asleep because he didn't know he was asleep. Then he would start to fall asleep again.

"Hey. These people are looking at me funny," I complained.

He opened one eye at a time. "WHO?" He was ready to fight, or maybe just be polite to visitors.

"Those two," I said as I pointed to the picture on the wall. He relaxed a little and rubbed his eyes.

"Those are your great grandparents, Flavio," he said as he sat up with a little more pride in his voice. He brushed his Pancho Villa mustache with his hand and looked every bit as though he were getting ready for something important.

"So is that your *mamá y papá,* or *abuelita's?*"

"Mine."

"Where did they come from?" I lived to wonder why I asked.

"I will tell you, but you must listen quietly because this is very *interesante.*" He got up and put another *piñon* log in the fire and sat back down in his chair. "In the high mountains to the *norte,* two great rivers are born. From the left comes the Rio Chama, which is in the land of the Ute. From the right comes el Rio Grande, which is born high up in the San Juan mountains and runs down steep canyons until it enters the Valle de San Luis. There it is peaceful and serves the people well; but then it suddenly falls into a very deep canyon and for a long distance it tumbles white in the rocks until it finally comes out at Velarde ready to meet its brother, the Chama. Where the two rivers meet is a very important place because that is where the people in the picture were from. They are part *indio* and part *guachupín.* The *indio* has been there forever, but the *guachupín* came from far away; from Spain. The two peoples made a very strong race, both very wise and very brave."

"Does that mean that I am wise and brave?" I asked, ready to be proud.

"No. It only means that you can become wise if you work very hard and learn all that nature can teach you. You will be brave when you are no longer afraid of death. But you must prove yourself. Right now you are just a rancher. That's all. And it is time for the first feeding of the stock." He grinned and pointed his heavy finger at me, and I knew I must work hard to earn my place in his eyes.

We stepped out into the daylight. The first snow of the fall had come to Capulín. Already the ground was nearly covered white. I followed El Grande's footsteps up the hill, past the outhouse and down toward the wooden gate that opened into the *vega* of pig fame. We could see cattle, sheep, and horses gathered around the haystacks beyond the *vega,* waiting and licking their chops. How they knew we would come I'll never know. Maybe the old ones told the young ones.

With the hay saw, El Grande made the first cut at the haystack, like taking the first slice of a giant loaf of bread. My job was to throw the hay over the fence to all the drooling mouths around the corral. The cows just shoveled it in and worried about chewing later. The horses bit and chewed as they went, taking their time because nobody pushed them around. The sheep sneaked here and there when the big animals weren't looking. And the goats thought they owned the whole *rancho.* It was hard work, but feeding the hungry, even in the middle of a snowstorm, made my heart feel good. I had to like it; it was done twice a day from now until spring.

Pitchfork still in my hand, I saw a rider on a black horse headed toward us. His hat covered his face from the snow, so I couldn't see who it was.

"It is your Tío Maclovio," El Grande said right away.

"How do you know?"

"I know the horse."

We waited for him to come up close.

"Buenos días, Don Ezequiel," he said as he rode to a stop next to the log fence. Then I could tell it was Tío Maclovio. He wasn't really my Tío, but in Capulín almost everybody was related, so to be respectful we called everybody *tío* or *tía*. "I have some very bad news," he said as he pulled up next to us. "We just got word that Rosa Velásquez died sometime during the night. Malvino stopped me on the road and gave me the news this morning on my way from *el puerto."*

"Rosa Velásquez!" El Grande repeated. I watched his face as it went from cold to serious.

We headed back to the house in a hurry. When we got close we could see that already some of the men were hanging around the store, waiting. El Grande went into his house, got his new hat and the 30-30, and headed to the store. I followed.

For as long as I could remember, it had been said that Rosa Velásquez was a witch. They said that she kept a devil doll and a special set of needles that she used to put curses on people she didn't like. The story about her turning into a coyote was the one that made me and the guys run whenever we saw her limping along the road with her crooked cane. Many years ago, it was told, a man had spotted a coyote along the edge of the forest. He fired a shot and hit it on the leg and the coyote limped off into the woods making sounds like a crying woman. The next day Rosa turned up with a broken leg. The man who had shot the coyote suddenly got very sick and finally killed himself with the same gun. And when we didn't behave, our parents threatened to send for Rosa Velásquez.

"¿Ya saben lo que pasó?" he asked the men as we came up to the porch. They all nodded yes. In his *mayordomo* voice he said he would have to investigate. Bernabé would drive him to the old woman's shack. When he was official, nobody asked questions. We all stood on the porch of the Capulín Cash Store as we watched them drive up the hill in the old pickup truck toward the shack where the witch lived.

For the next two days Rosa Velásquez was the only thing to talk about at school. We wondered if everything we had heard was true. José Torres, the toothy kid, said he knew all about witches—how to defend yourself and how to kill them. If you wrapped yourself with a rope of horsehair you were safe. If you needed to kill one, you had to make a cross on the bullet. And if one put a curse on you, you had to find a *curandera* who would make you a special tea from herbs, bugs, blood, and maybe a little sugar to kill the taste. Mrs. Majors said there was no such thing as witches. Rosa Velásquez was a poor old woman who acted a little strange, she said. Then she told us about the Salem witches and we all sat glued to our desks. Finally she explained that it was the Salem village people who had turned evil, not the women hanged for being witches.

But José Torres knew better. "In Capulín we have them," he said from the back of the room, a little mad. "And if you say there are no witches, the witches get mad, so you better watch out, dear teacher. Who wants to learn fractions from somebody with a curse?"

Everybody laughed.

"Enough of this! There are no witches, and that's that. You people are just backward," she said, her white face turning red.

We turned a little more brown.

On the night of the wake, El Grande got ready early. When I asked him if I could go with him he said it was fine, but I would have to come back alone because he had to stay until sunrise. The *velorio* was to be at the house of Tío Samuel, who lived on the ridge beyond the *vega,* overlooking the whole valley. It was not a short walk.

"Was Rosa Velásquez really a witch?" I asked him as we walked through the dim light of the *vega*, past the pig baths.

"No one knows for sure," he answered. After a little while he added, "Before the night is over we will know." Cold chills ran through my body. I wanted to ask more questions but he said that on such a night, it was better to keep quiet. Besides, I was going to have to walk back alone.

People were arriving from all directions by pickup trucks, horses, and foot. A big fire had been built near the house and all the men were standing around it. The women, all dressed in black, were in the house sitting in a big circle around the casket. Three candles at the head of Rosa's body and the light of the bonfire were all that lit the room. El Grande and I walked into the room to pay our respects to the dead woman. It smelled like strong perfume. Nobody was talking. At first I didn't dare to look at Rosa's dead face. But as I came around to her side I couldn't help it; I looked at her. Her face was like worn-out leather, ugly. I remembered having seen her on the road; we had hidden from her in the weeds. A witch, powers, able to hand out the curses, the fear of everyone—and there she was, in a wood box, dead. Was it for sure? Maybe it was just a little step to something else. Another coyote? There were no flowers, no rosaries, and no crosses.

As we walked back out, I saw a pair of big scissors that had been hung over the door.

Outside, the chatter of the men around the fire filled the cold, dark night. Millions of stars covered the sky, some twinkling, some not. Little dim lights down in the valley were all that told where the village of Capulín was this night. El Grande, keeper of the peace, was now sitting on a bench near the fire, with his hex-barrel 30-30 Winchester rifle across his lap. All the old *tíos* sat near him, *platicas* back and forth but in a low voice, not wanting to make anything in the night air think they were disrespectful. Out near the trucks some of the other men were talking and passing the bottle around. *"Pa' calentarnos,"* I heard one say with a giggle. Malvino and I stood off by ourselves watching the slow action around the fire. I wondered why he had been the first to know that Rosa Velásquez was dead.

The cold night wore on. A big orange moon had started up behind the deep forest and long shadows began to finger out toward the village. Coyotes howled from every direction. Owls, too, joined the crackle of the fire. The quiet chatter of the men died to whispers, the whiskey and the load of the day were now part of the mood.

¡MIREN! ¡MARIA ¡PURISIMA! Somebody screamed. It was Pedro pointing to the forest. Then we all saw it. A fire like a torch spitting sparks moving fast through the oak thickets, into the *chamisal* and then up the ridge and beyond into the *vega* and out of sight. It had moved fast, hopping as it went. We stood stunned. The sleeping dogs woke up, barking wild. Not a sound from the coyotes, and the cool breeze was silent. *"¡A la madre!"* I heard someone say. Others started to repeat the names of the saints. Even some of the women inside had seen it. They prayed to whatever saint was handy. What was it, and will it come back? I wondered as I shivered.

"Pues, ya nos dijo," El Grande finally stood up and said, official like. Then everybody stood up, waiting for him to say what to do next. Rifle now in both hands, El Grande walked toward the door of the *velorio.* We all followed. The women were quickly looking for their belongings and wrapping themselves up in black things. He and two men reached into the casket and turned the body on its face. Then the casket was closed and nailed shut. The men lifted the box with Rosa Velásquez and loaded it on a pickup truck near the fire. People were hurrying everywhere. The men hopped the first ride they could reach. The women headed home. I was standing near the door wondering if I should hop a ride or walk home the way I had been told. Just then my mother and Mama Grande grabbed me at the same time. "You come with us." I didn't argue. We got into our Ford pickup truck, La Grande in the middle and my mother driving, and headed down the little dirt road toward the main road that would get us home, thanks to God.

"Did you see it? Do you want to know what I saw?" I asked.

"NO! We already know what happened," La Grande said with a quick look my way. "There are some things you are still too young to understand. Be happy with your innocence."

Happy with my innocence? What did she know, I thought. Was there something about witches even more terrible than what I knew? Were La Grande and my mother trying to protect me from something evil?

"But maybe it was just a shooting star, or somebody pulling a prank. Maybe we should go look where it went....in the morning," I said bravely. They didn't answer.

We pulled up in front of the store. My mother left the truck running with the lights on. "You walk La Grande across the road to the door. Come right back," she ordered in her short voice. I held La Grande's warm, leathery hand tight as we walked across the dirt road and up the board walk to the door of the house. I said good night and she blessed me. On my way back I stopped where I had a clear view of the *vega,* between the thickets, where the fireball had headed. In the light of the moon I could see a few patches of water shining bright. The long shadows of the chokecherry thicket looked like giant fingers reaching across the land toward me. The coyotes were having excited *pláticas* of their own. Now and then an owl said something far off in the *monte,* too. The bright night was filled with a cold mist and all the shadows seemed to be moving. And somewhere in the deep forest, Rosa Velásquez was being buried before dawn, face down.

SEIS

"Hadedusa."

"Hadidusah."

"Hadidusa."

"Buenos días, Grande," I said as I went into the shed. He was busy talking to himself and mending a horse harness. "What were you saying? It sounded Indian." I joked him because he always talked to himself. Sang to himself, too. His favorite little tune sounded like something between a hymn and a coyote.

"¿Yo? Yo no dije nada." He frowned.

"You were saying something like 'hadidusa' or something," I pushed.

"¡Qué chamaco!" He growled. I jumped back. Then he grew thoughtful. "Ok, I was practicing my English. The *americanos* say something like that when they greet you. You know English. What is it?"

"There is no English like that! But if you'll write it down I'll run across the road and ask *mi mama,"* I said, ready to help.

"¡Chamaco sonso! If I can't speak it, how can I write it?" He had a point. Sometimes I got a little ahead of myself.

"Why do you need to practice English, anyway?"

"Me and some of the men are going over this morning to talk with the *gringos;* the ones that are laying out the new molino. I don't think they speak Spanish so we are taking Roberto. But I sure would like to show them I can speak some English, too." He looked a little worried. *"Malditos gringos,"* he muttered under his breath.

"I'll go. I'll talk for you. I can even say stuff like, 'go to hell,'" I said proudly. "If we need it, I mean." I remembered the woodpile from the last time I had used the words.

"No! No! No!" he shouted. He pointed his finger at me and squinted one eye. That meant I should quit trying, for now.

Later that morning the men gathered around the potbelly. All the talk was about the new sawmill. Bernabé Archuleta arrived in his new GMC, baby shoes hanging from the rearview mirror. A nude woman was buried in the clear plastic gearshift knob. You could see everything! Bernabé had been in the war where they had found a lot of people starving and getting put into ovens to burn. He had come back with many stories about some *maldito* named Hitler; a German guy who everybody was afraid of. Since Bernabé's dog was German, too, he had named it after Hitler just so he could have something to kick when he thought badly about being in the war. So in Capulín, the dog paid for the war, and when Bernabé drove up in front of the gas pump, our three mangy dogs barked and growled at Hitler who stood proudly in the back of the truck. Then the dogs peed on the tires as a sign of welcome to the Capulín Cash Store. From the other side, Isaias Martínez, who owned most of the Capulín Bar, drove up. Soon came Pedro driving his Farmall tractor, with Malvino sitting on the plow. Roberto walked since he was close. His two dogs also had a few words for all the others.

There was no way I was going to miss any of the meeting with the *gringos,* so I sat on the porch watching the action as El Grande came across the road wearing his new hat and carrying his hex-barrel 30-30 in his arms. He was dressed for business.

"Buenos días, Don Ezequiel," they all said as he walked in.

"¿Que los gringos comen perro?" he asked. They all laughed. *"Pues, aquí les llevamos lonche!"* he added as he looked at all the dogs through the window. They all laughed again. His little joke about *gringos* eating dog was to get everybody to listen. Then El Grande got down to business. He said they would tell the gringos the mill was too close to the village and, actually, the people did not want it anywhere. They did not even want roads into the deep forest. All the big trucks would make too much dust and noise. Horses would spook. And the people of Capulín did not want outsiders moving to the village. All this he told Roberto to say and for the rest to back him up.

Somebody said that it was real *importante* that the community tell the *gringos* how it was going to be. Somebody else wanted to run home and get some guns, but El Grande said no. The only gun was the hex-barrel. It was the law. What about the road already to the molino? Maybe they should tell them to tear it up. No, somebody else said. The men could use it to get wood from that part of the mesa. By now the men were getting real pushy and ready for *chingasos* if the *gringos* got smart.

While all this was going on inside the store, I sneaked out, jumped into the back of the GMC with Hitler, and hid under a tarp that Bernabé carried for the dog to lie on. The dog tried to dig me out, but I kicked at him and he quit. Soon the men hurried out and got into the two trucks. Pedro and Malvino back on the tractor. Pickups, tractor, and dogs headed up the hill from the store toward the dirt road that led to the new sawmill. Hitler kept stepping on me, but I was just happy nobody had found me.

The big cloud of dust caught up as the trucks rolled to a stop in front of a metal shed. There were some huge yellow machines, bigger than the ones the *eléctricos* used. At the edge of the clearing was a big tank with PHILLIPS 66 in orange letters written on one side. The whole place smelled so good—like diesel.

"Holy shit, Jake! They got guns!" I heard a man with a raspy voice yell. I peeked out and saw El Grande and Roberto standing near the truck. One man walked slowly out of the building, hands on his hips, while others watched from the door. He looked like he was Mrs. Majors' brother. "How do you do, sir," he said as he walked toward El Grande.

"Hadidusa," El Grande said as he touched his hat.

"That's a mighty fine ole gun you got there, *amigo*, but you don't need it here, please," the *gringo* said.

"Mucho bueno pa'l vena'o," El Grande said as he pointed it at a fake deer in the sky. Everybody smiled uneasy.

"What can we do for you fine gentlemen?" the *gringo* asked.

"We hear youse gonna put up here a sawmeal," Roberto said in a deep macho voice.

"Yup. This here mill's goin'ta belong to the Duke City Lumber Corporation. Me'n the boys here are under contract to build it." Then the *gringo* told them it would operate for years and there would be many jobs for the community and for people who would come to live at the sawmill. Roberto said everything again in Spanish for El Grande.

"Dis *molino* too much close to da community, Capulín," Roberto said as he pointed over his shoulder toward the village.

"Why, we're doin' that on purpose. So ye'all can git to work on time," the man said with a laugh. Everybody smiled a little.

Suddenly, out of the dust came a clanging noise and the sound of an engine. It was Pedro. He jumped off the tractor. Malvino followed. Pedro tipped his hat to the *gringos* and then explained to El Grande how Malvino had fallen off the tractor and gotten stuck in the rails of the cattle guard. It took a while to get him loose.

"Eres como las vacas de Emilio," El Grande said, laughing as he pointed to Malvino. The men laughed. The *gringos* smiled. Malvino paid no attention. He spotted the mangy German Shepherd in the back of Bernabé's truck and hopped over to pet him. Hitler was not used to kindness. Like most dogs that have been kicked around, Hitler peed when you petted him.

"Yakaaa-Peeuu!" I yelled as a river of dog pee ran along a crease in the tarp and down my neck. Hot, too. Tarp flew, and I jumped off the truck, pulling off my shirt. All the other dogs started barking. Malvino, a grown man, started crying. I didn't care. I looked up to see all the men laughing, some even bent over. One was on his knees to keep from falling over. El Grande stood stone-faced, rifle in one hand, hip in the other. I knew I would soon be dead.

"Hey kid, dog piss don't do nothin' but turn yore hair yella." The *gringos* laughed even more. "I've heard of dogs smelling you out, but never peeing you out." More laughs.

I looked for a sign from El Grande.

"You boys sure perked things up 'round here. Ah swear, I never laughed so hard in my life. Why don't ye'all come on into the shed here and take a few pulls off of Jake's Yukon Jack," the *gringo* said.

"Que nos quiren dar un traguito," Roberto explained. El Grande looked around, then motioned to the truck with the rifle.

"Está bien," he said as they all headed toward the shed. I was to sit in the truck and dream about my coming meeting with the leather *reata.* Malvino stayed with me, no doubt to do his own dreaming.

"Cómo eres pendéjo. You are going to get me killed," I said to Malvino. He didn't really listen. "Are you really crazy like they say?"

"No. Hell, no. I'm not crazy." He growled at me for a minute. "I have been blessed by God with a special power."

"Liar! Like what power?" He was making me madder.

"I can see things and hear things no one else can. I go away for special schooling. The government wants to know more about my powers because they will need me when the war starts again."

"Liar. You go to the place for the insane, the nut house," I yelled at him. "OK. What things can you see?" I added. For a little while he didn't say anything.

"They are all in there drinking whiskey," he mumbled.

"Is El Grande drinking, too?" I asked, sarcastically.

"Yes."

"Ahaa! Now I know you're crazy. El Grande would never touch the stuff. They're lucky he even let them take a drink. You're crazier than hell!" I yelled.

Malvino wouldn't talk to me anymore, but at least now I knew that he was really crazy, making up stories and laughing to himself. I sat in the truck, waiting and trying not to look at Bernabé's gearshift knob, but every now and then I sneaked a little look. As the afternoon dragged by I tried to picture what the *molino* would be like. How did the *gringos* know all that stuff? About to go to sleep, I heard them all laughing. When I opened my eyes they were staggering out of the shed. Pedro was first, next a *gringo,* then I couldn't tell. They were drunk for sure.

Then I saw him. Bernabé was holding him up on one side and Jake the other. El Grande looked like a dead bear with a hat. He was drunk. I felt sick and wanted to cry. Maybe I'm just dreaming, I thought. But when they brought him around to my side of the truck I could see his mouth open and spit dripping down his chin. I got down from the seat and held the door open. They loaded him just like he and Pedro had loaded Mrs. Majors a long time ago. I didn't know what to think. What had happened? What about the meeting, the *molino?* It looked like nobody cared anymore.

The line of trucks, tractor, and dogs snaked out of the molino while the *gringos* laughed and waved good-bye. When we got back home, Bernabé backed his truck up to the door of the cellar behind the tool shed. We unloaded El Grande, took him into the dark cellar, and sat him down on a big pile of empty gunny sacks. Bernabé told me to watch him until he sobered up. Then he drove away, quickly. I closed the door until there was just a little slit of light, enough to see if he was breathing. Then I sat down to wait. I wondered what it must be like to be really drunk.

"Agua." He sounded sick. I found an empty jar and ran to the well, hoping nobody would see me. What would I say? I have a drunk bear back in the potato cellar that is asking for a little water? I gave him some water, and he went back to sleep.

In the late afternoon, he finally woke up. He sat up and shook his head, but didn't say anything. I was just sure the *gringos* had some kind of power to make good people get drunk.

"Yooohuuu." It was La Grande looking for him. "Ezequiel. Ehhzehquiell... *'onde estás... ya está la comida."* I didn't dare answer. She would never understand. But in the next instant, I heard her walk right up to the cellar door. "Yoohuu." No answer from the darkness. *"¿Onde 'stá ese viejo?"* I heard her say as she turned away. Close!

He reached over and grabbed my arm. "This is very bad. What you have seen today, you will never tell a living thing. Do you understand?" he asked. He was very serious. I promised him it would be our secret. For the first time in my life he shook my hand, like he did with the men.

Confused, I walked toward the creek still wondering what had gone wrong. Were they going to build the *molino?* Was it true that all the men would go to work for the Duke City Lumber Corporation? At the creek I tried to wash the smell of Hitler off my body as best I could. But not good. I sat on a little patch of grass, still smelling like dirty dog. Since El Grande couldn't answer the questions, the only one left was God. I looked to the sky and asked Him a few questions. Then I waited, and waited. *¡Nada!*

With the first stars of night already twinkling, not sure of anything, not even God, I headed home.

SIETE

The *gringos* came to the store almost every day. They always asked me how my grandfather was doing, with a little smile showing their tobacco-brown teeth. Sometimes they even dared to asked if my hair was turning yellow yet. I just smiled, shy. El Grande never came over to the store when the *gringos* were there. He said they didn't know how to talk to him, so no use making them feel bad. Besides, when the Capulín winter came, they would forget about the molino and leave. He said that no *gringo* could stand that kind of cold for very long. I knew he was right because I could barely take it myself.

It was the sixteenth of December. Every year on this day, El Grande headed into the deep forest to cut three Christmas trees: one for his house, one for ours, and one for the store. It was a weekday and I begged my mother to let me be sick so I could skip school and go with him.

"If I let you be sick, when your father finds out you will really be sick," she educated me one more time.

"But how would he find out? Who would even tell him?" I asked *razonablemente.*

"Me." *Tan, tan.* That was the end of that song. It wasn't that I liked cutting trees so much. And I didn't mind going to school on the sixteenth of December. It was that I wanted to talk to El Grande about the luminarias and the *abuelo,* maybe get a little inside information.

It was tradition. For the nine days before Christmas all of us boys had to show up at the *luminarias* and answer to the *abuelo,* the boogie man we paid up to for the year past. And he remembered everything. For the whole year, when any of us did bad, the *abuelo* was thrown at us as the no-mercy judge you would have to answer to at Christmas time. El Grande always seemed to know what the *abuelo* would be like every year—mean or easy. Sometimes I wondered if he was really the *abuelo.* For this year, I would have to wait and find out what mood he was in by the fire.

Christmas had come to our adobe school with an extra load of no-homework. Mrs. Majors liked drama, so she did away with arithmetic, all the adverbs, and Dick and Jane. What we got for two weeks were decorations everywhere and the Christmas play. It was about some cowboys down Texas *Méjico* way celebrating Christmas around the campfire, making the best of the worst. I was Pancho, the only Pancho north of the rio and a good sidekick to the smart cowpokes from this side of the border. I already knew my lines, but I had trouble sounding like Mrs. Majors said Mes'kin cowboys sounded. I figured that the Capulín sound was all we needed, but she was looking for something even better. We were the only Mexicans I had ever heard and all of us were cowboys, mas o menos. So what more can you ask? I wondered.

Toward the end of the play, all the cowboys sat around the fire singing about silent night while one of us picked the guitar. When the song was over I was supposed to stand up, walk around a little, lift my hat and scratch my *piojos* and say, "Whatt I guant for creesmess *es* a bottle of tequila, some beans and chile and lots of beautiful *señoritas.*" Not a bad creesmess as creesmesses go around our house. Anyway, all the other cowboys were supposed to laugh and say, "Oh, Pancho!" Then I was to grab the guitar, walk the strings twice and sing, *"Noche de paz, noche de amor, todos duermen al redor..."* and then motion to the community to sing along with all the sad cowboys. When the song was over, Christmas was over at the school. But no way was that the end to the pain ahead of us.

The *luminaria* in Capulín was none of that candle-in-paper-bag stuff. It was a big fire of thick boards, logs, old tires, and even parts of the poles from the R.E.A. And the talk around school was enough to scare even El Grande. One kid said he heard that one year the devil himself had jumped out of the fire. Another one said that the *abuelo* could read your mind. The big story was about the kid who was sent by the *abuelo* to bring back a list of the names on the stones in the *campo santo.* He was in the cemetery for hours trying to read the names on the tombstones. When he finally came back to the fire, his hands and his list were covered with blood.

"*¡A la madre!* I think I'm going home and get sick," said Ricardo as he held on to his own elbows.

"The *abuelo* can't make me do that," Lorenzo, the ape kid, said, all cocky.

"How come?" we all said like one voice.

"Because I can't read." Everybody laughed a little bit.

Then José Torres, the sixth-grader, spoke up. "I'm gonna tell the *abuelo* that all of youse guys are chicken chit," he said his big yellow teeth flashing. "He gets worsen when he knows you are scared," he smiled again.

With everybody pretending not to be scared, we headed home from school thinking about the coming night. I ran down into the deep arroyo and up the other side trying to remember all the evil things I had done. The big one was what I had said to Mrs. Majors on the first day of school a long time ago. The *abuelo* would never forget that one.

"Where did you get the big mustache?" my mother asked as I came into the Capulín Cash Store where she was standing by the potbelly.

"When I am Pancho the Mes'kin caboy from south of the Rio Grande celebrating creesmess with my *gringo* friends around the campfire, sad but thinking of tequila and all the beautiful *señoritas* I have known in my times, I have to have this beard," I said, forgetting the *abuelo,* lost in the romance. I think Mrs. Majors had done a good job with me.

"Pancho better get on his horse and head for the woodpile. His chores must be done early because tonight at seven he must ride into the hands of the *abuelo* where the campfire is very big and the mercy is very, very tiny." I couldn't believe it was my own mother saying those things. Didn't she care? From cowboy to coward in a flash, the wild and who-cares Pancho was on his way to the woodpile to cut wood for the night, with his *pistola* shrunk down to size. Mothers can do that to you.

A little after supper, El Grande brought two beautiful trees to the porch of the store. He was proud because he thought the deep forest had made them just for him. He came in the house and sat down at the table to talk; the electric poles were already deep into the forest and there was a lot of snow piled up. He hardly even looked at me. I worried about the big night with the hairy monster across the bridge. One thing began to worry me even more: If El Grande was the *abuelo,* he sure was slow about getting his scary suit on. While he and my father shared a little *platica,* I put on my heavy wools for extra padding. When you're scared you gotta stay busy. I was overworked until almost seven.

"¡Pues, ya es tiempo!" he announced in his *mayordomo* voice. At once I needed to pee. But no big going away *fiesta.* My mother just opened the door, as though to put the cat out for the night, and said to be careful. I wanted to believe she knew enough that she didn't need to say more. I figured El Grande

would sneak out right after I left and put on his *abuelo* suit. When you're scared you lie to yourself, too.

It was a black night with no moon to be found. I walked down the dirt road toward the bridge. When I got close I could hear some of the guys talking. "Hey, Pancho, are you scared or what?" somebody asked as I came up. They had started calling me Pancho because of the play.

"Naw. I ain't. What about you?"

"Chale. What is there to be afraid of," Leo said todo brave. Ricardo's elbows were almost glowing in the dark.

"I wouldn't say that, *pendejos.* The *abuelo* hears everything. He knows everything. Youse guys are *estúpidos,"* José reminded. Nobody argued. We just stood around talking, with our little worries to ourselves, kicking rocks off the bridge and down into the water. Waiting.

Finally a pickup truck came down the road loaded with what looked like big logs and tires. Near the bridge it turned off the road toward a sandy part near the water. The driver hollered for us to run down and unload fast. We made a big pile out of all the stuff he had. Another man came around and lit it. About the time the fire started to grow, another truck rolled up to the bridge and slowed down. We saw some kind of animal jump off. In no time we knew it was no regular animal; it was the *abuelo!* He ran to the fire, cracking a long whip. He had long hair all over his body. White ribs were painted on his chest. His face was like a skull with hair. He had a long, stiff tail and growled like a mad dog. He was fast, too. I knew then it wasn't El Grande. He ran around the fire once and headed across the creek and under the bridge where we couldn't see him. We waited, but he wouldn't come out.

Abuelo or not, we decided to dig him out. Braver in a group, we worked our way near the bridge and called to him, "Come here, *abuelo, abuelo."* No answer. "Hey. Are you going wee wee or what?" *Nada.* "We have your lunch over here waiting... we give you Lorenzo to eat." Nothing. We got tough. "If you don't come out, we'll tow you out with your whip, *señor abuelo."* But we were not that brave. Finally, one of the men standing around the fire came up to us and told us to go home. The fire was dying down. "Sometimes the *abuelo* waits a night so he can get really mean. Remember, you still have eight nights to go," he said.

Making jokes about the chicken *abuelo,* we headed home happy, but already thinking about the next night.

School was out for vacation, so in the late afternoon we all had a little *junta* on the porch of the store. Everybody had an idea. Somebody had heard the *abuelo* had fallen into the deep pool under the bridge and drowned in the dark. Somebody else said, you wish. Another said that the *abuelo* was a giant hairy frog—*una ranota*. But José Torres was a *veterano* of many *luminarias,* so he knew for sure. "You just wait. What we saw last night is going to be one mean *abuelo.* I can tell. He has a new whip and last year he was easy. This year some of youse will prob'ly die." We all looked around trying to guess who it was. I secretly hoped it was José, or maybe the ape kid. We agreed we would meet at the porch at seven and walk down to the bridge together.

By the time we were all at the bridge again that night, all the bravery was gone. We stood around spitting and covering it with our foot. Nobody talked. This time the pile of wood was already there, but nobody had seen who did it.

"LOOK! *¡A LA MADRE!"* Ricardo screamed, pointing to the other side of the creek: The *abuelo*, running about fifty m.p.h. through the *chamisal* with a burning torch. He dropped down the riverbank, into the water, and out the other side to the woodpile. We could just barely see him with the light of his torch as he danced around, screaming as though in pain. He lit the pile on all sides. Then, like lightning, he headed to the bridge, torch in one hand, cracking whip in the other. *"A la lumbre,"* he growled. Like moths, we ran to the fire. He looked just like he had the night before, but now he was wearing white gloves to match his ribs. He could jump high in the air, run from one side to the other faster than any of us, and he moved like he had joints everywhere. We stood in a tight group on one side of the fire. He looked at us through the fire from the other side.

"One by one come to me," he ordered. We all shoved the person standing next to us, but nobody went. "He who is most afraid, come," he now said with a kind voice. Lorenzo quickly stepped up to him.

"What is your name?" he asked as he gave the ape kid a quick swat with his whip.

"Lorenzo."

"You mean Lorenzo, *señor abuelo,"* and another stiff swat.

"Yes. Lorenzo, *señor abuelo."*

"Go. Bring me the next victim," he ordered as he gave him one more. We all tried to get invisible. I was closest and the ape kid delivered me by the arm. The *abuelo* asked my name and I answered politely. I got a stinging swat like nothing the leather *reata* hanging in the smokehouse had ever handed out.

"Are you afraid of me?" he asked, spitting.

"Yes, *señor abuelo."* Crack! It stung more than the first one.

"Last night you were yelling, saying you were not afraid of me. You are lying to me," he growled.

"No, *señor abuelo.* That was last night. Now I am afraid," I tried to make sense. He sent me away to think and to get the next kid with one last swat.

Each of us took his turn. He found something wrong with what everybody answered, which was even worse than Mrs. Majors. Next he lined us up and made us prance around the fire singing, "The *abuelo* is a chicken, the *abuelo* is a chicken," and as we came around each one got a swat. Then he invented other games, all ending up in a swat. Suddenly out of the darkness, one of the older men who had been watching grabbed the *abuelo* from behind, took his whip, and ran into the *chamisal*. The *abuelo* chased him and soon we heard screams from the dark. After a short while the abuelo trotted back to the fire with his whip and blood around his mouth and on his hands.

"Does anyone else dare to get stupid?" he asked with a big red smile. We stood like stumps. He looked us over, waiting for an answer. But the stumps didn't move. Then he cracked his whip, laughed real ugly, and walked away toward the bridge.

For the rest of the nights of *luminarias* there were no dropouts. The *abuelo* showed up every night, too; and a bigger and bigger group of old men came to watch. All the bad things we had done came out, as though some sneaky reporter had followed us around all year writing things down. The abuelo wasn't as dumb as he looked, either. The first few nights it was all swats and fear, but as the nights passed he started sounding more like El Grande, asking questions and giving lessons. We got more cocky, too. We played little tricks on him and sometimes he didn't even know it. You might even say it was getting to be fun.

It was finally Christmas Eve, the last night. Every night he had come running from a different place, but tonight he came down the road on a beautiful black horse with a fancy saddle, and a big pack strapped to the back. He chased us around the fire a few times and then made us sit down. He turned to the old men and asked if anyone had a complaint, a *queja*. This was their chance to get us.

Tío Casimiro came forward. "Last summer I caught one of them stealing eggs from my chicken coop," he said.

"That person will now step forward," the *abuelo* ordered. We all looked around, but nobody moved. "Then all of you will pay," the *abuelo* said, cracking his whip.

"Ok, Ok. It was me, *señor abuelo,"* the ape kid said as he stood up and went before the *abuelo.*

"How many eggs did you steal?"

"Twenty-two, *señor abuelo."* We all laughed.

"What did you do with them?"

"I boiled them in a bucket of water and ate them." Lorenzo smiled a little. The *abuelo* jumped back and held his nose.

"You must still be passing gas," he snorted. Everybody around the fire laughed. "Go over and blow them a big one; about five eggs worth," he said as he pointed to us. We held our noses and waved him away. Lorenzo bent over and tried, but nothing happened. WHACK! It was the hardest swat of the week. "Maybe that will help," the *abuelo* screamed. We started chanting, "We want a *pedo,* we want a *pedo.*" Finally the ape kid called for silence. It wasn't long but it had a nice deep tone; we all clapped. The *abuelo* leaned over and gave Lorenzo one final swat. "For the rest of your life, every time you fart you will remember not to steal," he said.

The *abuelo* called for other *quejas* and the men came up with a lot of them, some not even true. Everybody got a little sermon and a few swats. It was getting late and I knew it would soon be my turn. On the night before, I had been called to account for telling Mrs. Majors to go to hell. The *abuelo* himself remembered it and ordered me to write a letter to Mrs. Majors saying I was sorry. Tonight I was supposed to read it in front of everybody.

"Do we have any unfinished business?" the *abuelo* asked, looking a little tired. All the guys pointed to my head.

"I... I do, *señor abuelo,*" I confessed as I stood up and pulled a crumpled piece of paper from my pocket. He acted as if he didn't remember. "It is a letter to the teacher, Mrs. Majors. You told me to bring it tonight and read it." He made a quick turn and gave me a stinging swat.

"Well, read it, *muchacho,*" he said, *todo* sarcastic.

"Dear Mrs. Majors. I am sorry for telling you to go to hell. Hell is not a good place, not even for a teacher. I am glad you threw me across the room so I could learn a good lesson. I hope you are still my friend. Your friend, Pancho the Mexican caboy."

"Hee Hee." All the guys laughed and clapped. I felt ashamed.

"Was that good enough?" the *abuelo* asked everybody. Lucky for me, nobody complained. "All right, you lazy bums. Get up and line up here and get ready to recite and sing like I told you two nights ago." Suddenly he was extra mean again. We all jumped up and made a line facing the church up the hill. He cracked his whip and ordered us to march. Up the hill we went, goosing each other when the *abuelo* wasn't looking. He stopped us at the door of the church, told us again what he had told us to do when we marched in. Then he disappeared.

The doors to the church opened and we could see all the people sitting quietly, waiting for midnight mass to start. We marched in a straight line to the front and stood facing everybody who lived in Capulín.

Silent night, holy night
all is calm, all is bright.
Round yon virgin, Mother and Child
Holy infant so tender and mild.
Sleep in heavenly peace
Sleep in heavenly peace...
Noche de paz, noche de amor
Todos duermen en derredor
Entre los astros que esparcen su luz
Bella anunciando al Ninito Jesús
Brilla la estrella de paz
Brilla la estrella de paz.
Oremos, oremos
Angelitos semos
Del cielo venimos
A pedir oremos.
En Belen nació Jesús
Por ser hijo de María
Los señores como ustedes
Dan crismes en este día.

I could see El Grande with a big smile, sitting a few rows away. I knew he was proud that I had lived through the first *luminarias*. I felt proud, too, as when you pass to the fourth grade. As we marched out, I thanked God for El Grande and for Capulín. I could hear little whispers all over the church. When we got to the back of the church we found bowls of candy, nuts, and fruit. We filled our pockets and giggled.

Outside it was quiet. A million stars twinkled in the sky. The *abuelo* was gone. It was Christmas.

PARTE DOS

Transitions

OCHO

They picked the middle of winter, and it was cold. The Rural Electrification Administration threw the switch from somewhere far away. Capulín stepped blurry-eyed into the electric lights. Long gone was the war against progress; the birds sat on the wires and didn't die, and everything the movie had said over a year ago was coming true. The light poured out of everybody's windows, even in the daytime. People were putting away their oil lamps and the Coleman lanterns. You could almost hear the poor *lamparas* saying, "After all the years, this is what I get? A quick cleaning and into a dusty box?" Refrigerators, mixers, and toasters that had been sitting around collecting the fine caliche dust suddenly came to life. Music, from some guy named Benny Goodman, and good old time *rancheras,* blasted from every door. Even the Lone Ranger and Tonto seemed to get better at catching bandidos. At our house, the old wooden radio was put away; a little one the size of a battery took over the job of getting Mr. Morgan Beatty to us every night. The shiny toaster was placed where the flour can used to be, The new rule was: No tortillas in the toaster, just sliced bread. Sorry to say, the tortilla was never to be seen again. The noisy, old clock was taken to the attic. Now a little quiet one, with a second hand to show us how fast our lives were passing, became the keeper of Mountain Standard Time.

The Capulín Cash Store was lit up like a real business. All the years of dust and soot that had settled on things had to be cleaned up. When the men came over for their *pláticas* around the potbelly, my mother gave them ashtrays and told them not to spit on the floor anymore. She decided to have specials, so if you bought three horseshoes you could get the fourth one free. If your horse only had three legs, it was no bargain. The nails were extra. But nothing changed things more than the new freezer that had been sitting quietly in the middle of the store, locked up, full of boxes of candy and bubble gum, since summer. No more pouring of vanilla, sugar, and milk on a cup of snow. Now we had real ice cream. It came in small paper tubs with a little wood spoon stuck on the top. All the kids from the village came with pennies in their hot little hands to buy the stuff.

El Grande would have nothing to do with electricity. Most of the *veteranos* of the war against progress finally surrendered to the wives. One by one they had their houses wired and hooked up. No matter the nagging from La Grande and my mother, El Grande would not give in. My mother begged, even on her knees; La Grande was getting old, her eyes were bad, and she should finally have her life made modern. But El Grande held his ground. He told of the day when the people would become dependent on all the electric gadgets; they would forget how to build and fix the things necessary for life. Before too long they would be at the mercy of the R.E.A. and the *molino* and the U.S. *floresta.* Then their freedom and their spirit would be gone. Finally my mother quit speaking to him and he would not come over to the store. She said he was being a brat. I didn't know what I was supposed to do. There had never been a quiet fight like this before.

Winter had come, but the *molino* kept getting bigger. Huge trucks loaded with big machines came almost every day.

Roberto was hired as a log cutter, and before you knew it he had a chain saw just like the *gringos*. He was proud. He came over to the store to show the other men how the saw worked. It put our double-filo ax to shame. The giant *molino's* round saw whirred away day and night making boards for all the new houses. At school we dreamed of someday becoming log cutters, too.

El Grande had been right about one thing. Every day new ones came, some in trucks and others pulling trailers; chairs, tables, and mattresses sticking up over the top. Most stopped for gas at the Conoco gas pump in front of the store, so for me it was like the front row for current events. A lot of them had yellow hair.

I worked hard helping to fill their trucks and cars with gas, checking the oil and kicking the tires. Some wanted water in their canvas waterbags so I ran to the well and filled them. Once in a while one of the big *gringos* gave me a nickel for doing a good job. I was surprised by this. Who ever heard of getting money for doing your job?

Gringo-watching became the new excuse to go for a ride on a Sunday afternoon. People would pile onto a pickup and ride up and down the *molino* road, hoping to get a look at the funny people. It was like when Dick and Jane went to the zoo in our reading book; but we did it fancy, in trucks and cars.

It wasn't long before we were face to face with them everywhere we looked. On the first day of school they came dressed up, like they were going to church. They all had come from funny places, like Little Rock or Sweetwater or Texarkana. One kid came from a place called Tulsa, and since the kid looked like a prairie dog anyway, we named him *Tusa.* They all smelled funny, too; not a bad smell. A little like mustard. Some had blue eyes, so blue it looked like they had holes in their heads so you could see the sky. The way they talked made us laugh. For something far from where you were standing, they said, "Ouch yonder." "Can't" got to be "cain't" and what we always knew as "shit" became "sheat."

Before the *gringo* kids came, Mrs. Majors was a good teacher. She told us that her job was to keep us in school for as long as she could and teach us all she knew. Most important was to read and write and to know math through fractions. She even made us play little games at recess because she wanted us to know there was more to life than just Emilio's rams.

When the first few little *gringos* came to school, she was like a chicken who had just hatched a nestfull of eggs. She clucked around the school yard, teaching them all our names. She even made Federico change his name to Fred so the *gringo* kids could say it. Timoteo became Tim and she even tried to change Facundo, but then she decided not to. Sometimes we called him Fac-U anyway.

She started talking like the *gringo* kids, so pretty soon we couldn't understand her either. During discussion time she mostly let them talk. They got to tell about the places they were from and about their vacation trips. We never had vacation. They got to do the fun chores, like passing out the singing books and ringing the bell. We got to carry wood and stoke the stove. And finally one day she said we couldn't speak Spanish in the school yard. If we did we would get our butts paddled.

Telling stories in front of the class was good education, so one by one Mrs. Majors made us stand up and talk about our favorite thing. As if we had just one. One little girl with yellow hair and the holes in her head talked about going to the beach. The sand was warm and the waves came crashing. She got a nice tan. What's a tan? we wondered. Another kid talked about going to the circus. Elephants stood on one leg and lions jumped through a fire. There was popcorn and cotton candy, too. Not even Perro, my forever-gone lamb, could do that. When Mrs. Majors asked for the next *voluntario,* only the *gringo* kids raised their hands. She swept the room with her eagle eyes and finally pointed her chubby finger at me. For the first time I was ashamed to be from Capulín—no beach, no elephants, and our lions just ate sheep and disappeared. I had to come up with a good one.

"My favorite thing is to go to La Mesa, our mountain *rancho,"* I started. "There my Papa Grande plants many things, but lots of potatoes. We grow millions. We raise cows, too. In the spring we round up the calves and cut their balls off." The guys exploded with laughter. Leo fell off his desk. Mrs. Majors turned *azul.* After a little while, she said to go on. "There is only one thing really bad about La Mesa; there are a lot of bears. Last year a big black one came out of the woods and ate my little sister, Lydia." I sat down. The *gringo* kids all had their mouths open. The guys looked at me as though I was on my way to prison. Mrs. Majors walked over to my desk and rested her big knuckles on my book.

"Are you telling the truth?" she asked through her teeth.

"It's true, it's true," the guys covered for me at the same time.

"How come I never heard of it?"

"Because the bear ate her in Spanish," José Torres yelled from the back of the room. Everybody laughed.

"I am so very sorry to hear that happened, if it's really true," she said. "But if I find out you have been telling a lie, I'm gointa wup you good," she added, pointing her heavy finger at my throat.

Every kid who lived far from the school brought lunch. Only a few had fancy *loncheras.* Most brought it in five-pound lard pails. Almost everybody's lunch was the same: A jar of *frijoles,* a boiled potato and a tortilla or two. If you had a good mother you also had a *biscochito* with lots of burned sugar on top. The *gringo* kids were different. They brought tuna fish, or peanut butter and jelly sandwiches on sliced bread. Some even had little cans of weenies you opened with a key.

One day Lupita Apodaca was sitting on the doorstep of the school eating her *lonche,* her black braids wiggling with every chew. Suddenly, like a chicken-stealing hawk, the *gringo* kid we called Tusa swooped down on Lupita's lunch pail and flew away with her tortilla, already one little bite taken out of it. He pranced around the school yard with the tortilla hanging between his fingers. Before Lupita could even say give it back, he flipped it to another kid in a mean game of keep-away. Lupita cried harder. The *gringo* kids giggled. Like a dog with an instant case of *rabia,* I came flying and hit Tusa with my entire streaking body. We crashed to the ground. I got up and kicked him in the head, then in the face. Such pure hatred I had never felt before. Even I got scared of myself; so I started to cry. The kid was bleeding from his nose and teeth. He was trying to get up, holding his face in one hand. I was trying to decide if I should hit him again. Thanks to God, Mrs. Majors grabbed both of us by our necks and squeezed. She looked us over. When she saw Tusa's face she dropped me and took him into the school. I was told to follow. She took the rag she cleaned the blackboard with and wiped the blood off the kid's face. I could see his eyes were swelling up so he was starting to look like a frog. His lip was cut. I felt bad. But more importantly I knew I was in very deep trouble, again. When she was finished with Tusa she walked over to me with a disgusted look on her big red face. This time it was no thunderclap voice.

"You go home. Tell your mother what you done. She must come'n see me right away. You can not come back to school." Her voice was calm. I knew I would never see the inside of a school again.

Outside the guys were waiting, bug-eyed.

"¡A la chingada! ¿Qué pasó?" José Torres wanted to know, and the others had questions, too.

"Did she whip you?"

"Is the Tusa dead?"

"Did she throw you out of school?"

"If she did, can I have your pencil and your hole-punched paper?"

I didn't answer any of the questions. I just walked down the rocky trail toward the deep arroyo, maybe for the last time. Somehow I felt like something that had already happened was happening again. It was awful. And this time I would no doubt have to eat the leather *reata.*

I got to the bottom of the deep arroyo, my worries so heavy I decided to sit down and rest for a little while. As I sat on the damp *caliche* thinking bad things about myself, I saw a coyote on the other side of the arroyo. He was just standing there looking at me. I didn't move. You hardly ever see them in the day, I thought. It was just he and I alone. I got a little scared, but still I just stared. He licked his face. I let out a little squeaky whistle. He lifted his head. I froze again.

"Is that you, Rosa Velásquez?" I finally asked. He didn't answer. In a little while I asked again, "Is that you, Rosa, the dead *bruja* who they said turned into a coyote?" The animal squatted down and put his face between his paws, still keeping his eyes and ears pointed right at me. Was he waiting for more, or was that his answer in coyote talk? "If it is you, Rosa, I want to ask a little favor, as a *bruja,* I mean." The coyote didn't move. I went on. "They say *brujas* have powers, dead or alive. If you can, I would like for you to burn down the new *molino.* Nothing left. Someday I will do you a little favor. Just burn it all down." Then I leaned back against the *barranco* and waited for the coyote to do something. Finally he got up and very slowly moved toward me. I was getting very scared, but I could see he was scared, too. One careful step at a time, the coyote came up to me and smelled my foot. I wondered if I had clean socks. Now I was so scared I didn't dare move. This was no regular coyote. He scratched at the ground and I was sure he was getting ready to bury my body for when he got hungry. "SHOOO, COYOTE!" I yelled as I came up ready to fight for my life. The coyote didn't charge or jump back; she just turned and trotted downstream, around a sharp bend and out of sight. My heart was pounding. I was sure he was Rosa Velásquez. Would he do me the little favor I had asked? I didn't know for sure, but I knew he had listened to me. I had at least one friend, even if it was a *bruja.*

Rumalda Ortiz was in the store buying rubber boots. I didn't have to slam into my troubles right away. But you know how it goes when your luck is down. Before I knew it Rumalda was gone, boots and all.

"*¿Por qué 'stás aquí? ¿Qué paso?*" My mother had a way with questions. "*Aye.* Don't even answer me, *chamaco frega'o.* Go across the road and tell it to your Grande. I am having a bad day. *Doña* Rumalda needs the boots but she has no money." Just then I could kiss *Doña* Rumalda, even if she was old and had no teeth. She saved me for a little while.

El Grande was up on the hill near the sheep *corral* digging a ditch, no doubt to drain the snow melt toward the *vega.* I walked up to him and didn't even say *buenas tardes.* I just told him everything. If you're going to die anyway, sometimes it is better to hurry up and get it over with.

"*¿Sabes qué, hijo?* All the animals of the forest and the *chamisal,* it makes no difference, fight and kill only to protect or to eat. Only *el hombre* kills for hate. *Coraje.*" I thought he was about to tell me he was going to kill me because he hated me. But no. He went on. "Man is the only one who can feel hate. *El hombre* is very dangerous. *Peligroso.* That is why only the man who can control his hate deserves to live among the other animals. The teacher is right. If you cannot control your anger you cannot be in school, even with the new *gringo* children." He sat back on the dirt bank and didn't say more. He just looked up and down my face like when somebody wants to see your eyes and your teeth at the same time. I couldn't take it so I buried my face in my hands. Then he spoke again. "*El gringo* is different, *hijo.* He thinks that God put all things here for him to control. To tame. To use up until it is all gone. He thinks he can own all that he sees and he will work and use violence to get it.

"We are not that way. We have a soul. We know that all other things have a soul, too, that we must respect. Our fight is not with the world. We live as one with the land and the water and the wind and the animals. We use of the world only what we need. Our fight is within. We must learn to control ourselves. In that, there is honor. *¿Me entiendes?* The *gringo* kid thought the tortilla was his to take, even if it hurt Lupita. You thought it was not respectful to take it away. You used violence to right a wrong. You could have told the *gringo* kid how it is that we do things here in Capulín. If you use violence you cannot be any better than they are." Then he slowly stood up and went back to work.

I walked back down the hill and sneaked into the potato cellar wishing that he had just used the leather *reata* instead. I sat down in the dark to think. Alone.

NUEVE

Maybe it was God, or maybe just my mother doing her *politica,* but by Monday I was back in school. The school, no doubt had changed; José Torres, aka Joe, was no longer the sixth grade because now we had Susie Kimball. She was in sixth, too, and smarter.

There was no school past the sixth grade in Capulín, so if you wanted more you had to go to some other place. *Salsipuedes,* as they used to say. My oldest brother, Adrian, had finished school and had gone away to the Navy, and Dolores was in Duke City. Cordy, and Juan were away at the boarding school in Santa Fe. My father had said they had no choice but to get an education. This left only my little brat sister, Lydia, and me at home. So I was the last of the men to help El Grande with the work of the *rancho.* But most *importante,* it was also my time to go with El Grande on my first winter bear hunt.

El Grande knew the deep forest better than anyone else, except maybe God, who he said made it. For fifty years, El Grande had wandered in the *floresta,* fixing the springs so the water was collected in *canovas* for animals to drink, helping little animals with broken legs, or putting out fires that were started by lightning. If Mother Nature would have been blessed with a son, it would have been El Grande; she treated him like one, anyway. He could find plenty to eat where there was nothing. He could make fine arrows out of the black *pedernal* and he could make fire from the *ocote* of the cedar. He could look to the sky and tell you how tomorrow would be. But best of all, he knew all the animals of the *floresta* as if they were his brothers. You could hear the little ring in his voice when he talked about the *venado* and the *nutria* and the *gavilán,* but I think el oso, the bear, was his favorite relative.

El Grande never took more from the *floresta* than he gave back. He killed and he saved life. He took what he needed: Deer for *carne seca* and hides, bear for rugs, turkey for meat to eat and feathers for his arrows. There was never a shortage of *Tewas chalecos* and *chaparreras,* all made of fine leather. But he always said that the *floresta* was like the garden; if you take care of it you will always have plenty to eat.

Getting ready for the winter bear hunt was serious. Knives were honed, guns were cleaned, and the heavy wool longjohns were washed. Ropes and the big saddlebags were checked. Food like beans, *carne asada,* red *chile* and tortillas were packed in the saddlebags. El Grande checked the shoes on the big team horses to make sure they were tight. We would use the large horses because they could carry more, even a dead bear if we were lucky.

Friday I didn't have to go to school. Except for fever or somebody's burial, this would be one of the few days I would be allowed to miss school. When I woke up, El Grande already had the horses saddled and was loading all our *provisiones.* I ran across the road so full of happiness that I didn't even notice how cold it was. I was wearing some heavy clothes and, on top of everything, the sheepskin coat he had made for me from the hide of my beloved Perro. It made me a little sad to wear it, so I only put it on when I was very happy. On his horse he had strapped the old hex-barrel .30-.30 and on mine the new model 94 short-barrel .30-.30 Winchester. I was proud to get to use it. It was new and it kicked a lot. Papa Grande led his horse out to the gate and I followed on mine. Across the road, on the porch of the Capulín Cash Store, my mother appeared.

"Papa. I think he is too young to go in this cold," she said with a little beg in her voice.

"Ya es hombre." El Grande smiled back through his thick *pancho villa*, already laced with ice. I smiled too, but no *pancho villa* on me yet. She did not argue with us, but I could tell she was about to cry.

"You be careful, stay covered up, and do everything El Grande tells you. You hear? It is going to be very cold in the mountains. God bless you, *mi'jito.*" The bear hunt was all that I cared about, so her words were sweet but faint in my covered ears.

We rode up the dirt road past the turnoff to the *molino* and up to the shortcut through Pedro's land. At the place where we would pick up the old road that was only good for Bernabé's Dodge Power Wagon or El Grande's horse wagon, we found a dirt highway. El Grande stood on his stirrups to get a better look at what he could not believe. The *gringos* had built a road up his mountain to La Mesa and the upper *rancho.* How could they do it so fast? A month ago all there was were hoof tracks and wagon ruts. *¿Qué pasó?* we both wondered.

We followed the road up toward the snow line. The country looked so different from the new road; old landmarks gone. Finally, at the cliffs of the *cañoncito* the new road ended. I could tell El Grande was happy.

"Hijo. This is as far as they will ever get," he said in his low official voice. By the time we arrived at the cabin of the upper *rancho* the sun was setting and a cold wind was blowing. Saddles slid off fast and horses went into the corral. There was stored-up alfalfa for food, but water was frozen. We carried all our things into the cabin, built a fire on the big kitchen stove, and started melting snow; water for the horses

and for us. *Hijo de la chingada*, it was cold! We were so hungry we ate our beans and *chile* cold, and fast. Not until we were finished eating did El Grande talk.

"It is going to be a cold day tomorrow. Cold enough to freeze my breath on my *bigote*. More snow in the afternoon and into the night." The windows were rattling with the wind and the glass was already frosted over. I could make out little pictures of jungle plants, sunsets, and explosions on the window panes.

"How do you know?" I asked.

"The wind." He didn't even look up from his plate. *"Viene del norte."* Then he said that the horses had also told him and he smiled for the first time. *"Los caballos me hablan."*

"I think it's going to be a real hot day and all the snow is going to melt. The dandelions are going to bloom and the bears are going to come out of their dens and eat us," I said, getting smarter by the minute.

"Only the part about the bears is true," he said, pointing a spoon at me. He laughed a little. Then he was quiet again. For a long while he said nothing more, but suddenly he turned and looked mean. *"El oso alazán* is the biggest bear that ever lived. I am going to tell you about him." He leaned back on his chair. He said it was a bear he had trapped many years before. *El alazán* had a hump on his back which made him look different from all other bears and he was meaner than any other animal in the deep forest. On his hind legs he stood over eight feet tall and he was faster than a horse. The bear killed a cow and carried it off into the thick brush, whole. El Grande and Tío Casimiro tracked it for days, but the bear knew the forest better. For the rest of the summer he found signs of the bear: turned-over rocks, rotting logs ripped open, and claw marks high up on the pine trees.

Before too long the bear killed a second cow; it was time for El Grande to get tough. He had to set a trap. It was a heavy iron trap with big jaws and sharp steel teeth. On the very first night the huge bear was caught, but when El

Grande checked the trap, the bear and the trap were gone. Using his dogs he tracked the bear for days until finally they caught up to him. They found him high up on a pine tree, trap and all. From up high among the branches the bear growled. El Grande moved around to get a good shot with his trusty .30-.30. He fired three shots. Quick as the rain, blood ran down the trunk of the tree, but no bear fell. Finally, with a fourth shot, the bear let loose of his grip, but the long chain tied to the trap got wrapped around a branch and the dying bear was left hanging high up in the tree. El Grande had to ride all the way back home for a pack horse and an ax to cut the tree down. Two days later he finally got the bear and his trap.

"Ahi está el oso alazán," he said as he pointed to the worn rug on the floor of the bedroom. "No other *alazán* has ever been seen in all of these mountains. That one on the floor was the last one." He scratched his head and he seemed a little sad.

"That's good," I said. "All the really mean bears are gone. The ones we will hunt are easy *¿qué no?"*

"The ones we will hunt are smaller brown ones. They are not as mean, but they are very smart," he said. He explained how the mamas will have cubs every two years. The tiny cubs are only a few ounces when they are born in the winter in the den. But by springtime, when they come out, they are big enough to hold their own. "It is very *importante* to know if a den belongs to an *oso* or an *osa*. We would never kill an *osa*," he said, which made me feel good. He said he knew how to tell which ones were *oso* dens.

The night was full of bear dreams. El Grande snored all night, and in my sleep I thought I was hearing bear growls. It was cold, too. The long night dragged on, but finally it was time to get up. Before dawn we were dressed in all our heavies. We headed for the corral to saddle up. I thought I would freeze before we even got started, but by the time we were ready to go I had warmed up a little bit.

We rode across the *rancho* and up onto a long and skinny mesa. There we plowed through deep, soft snow for a long time. The horses were almost sweating in the cold from all the jumping they were doing. When it finally ended we picked up the trail into the deep woods where nobody ever went, hardly even in summer. The snow got deeper, the horses sunk to their bellies and I got colder. About the time I was starting to think that winter bear hunting was for somebody else, El Grande stopped and got off his horse. He built a quick fire of dead twigs and small dry branches off the spruce. I worked on bringing my toes and fingers back to life. My fingers did better than my toes. They felt like heavy rocks inside my boots. For a flash I even dreamed what heaven it would be to do fractions next to the potbelly at school.

We were at the edge of the trees. El Grande decided to leave the horses there and head out on foot up a very steep slope. The snow was thinner because the wind had no doubt blown it away. We puffed steam as if our faces were on fire and carried our guns, rope, and axe until we finally came to some rock cliffs. El Grande puckered his lips as though he were going to kiss something or maybe just whistle a tune. He looked all around and listened. The forest was very quiet except for a little wind whistling through the trees and the sound of my heart pounding. No birds, no rabbits, no deer, no other life but us and the horses. The whole *floresta* seemed to be asleep, but in the sky snow clouds were getting ready.

"Hay está," El Grande said suddenly, breathing hard. He pointed to a crack in the rocks just above us.

"Who is it?" I thought he was talking about somebody he knew.

"El oso." He climbed up to a pile of twigs, dead leaves, and small rocks at the bottom of the crack in the cliff. He picked up a handful and smelled it. "It is the bear I am looking for," he whispered, with a big smile. He told me to dig out as much of the pile as I could with my hands. He slid back down into the aspen forest. For a little while I thought he had left me

there, just me and his sleeping bear. But before long he was back with a long aspen pole. He worked his way up above the entrance of the den and I followed close behind. Who wants to be the winter meal of a sleepy, darting bear? I thought. He spent a few minutes poking down into the rocks with the pole. *"Ahi está mi oso,"* he said finally as he poked, now very serious. "Get me the gun, the big one." He pointed to the hex-barrel with one hand and held the pole in the little hole he had found with the other. I slid down and came back up fast, not sure what might come out from under the pile of trash. I handed him the gun. He laid it flat on the pole and aimed it in the same direction. BLAM! The quiet winter day exploded with the sound of the hex-barrel. An awful, low growl came from inside. Then came another noise, like a baby crying. He moved the pole a little and fired again. We both listened, as coyotes do for prairie dogs in a hole. Nothing. He waited for a little while. Then he started poking around and feeling for movement. He shook his head. *"Ya está muerto."*

Back down at the pile of stuff, he helped me dig away from the entrance until we had made a dog-sized hole into the den. Then he handed me the end of the rope with a slip-knot and told me to crawl into the den and tie it to the bear. He said it didn't matter where, just tie it. I looked at him. For a split moment I thought of saying something I had said to Mrs. Majors a long time ago. But not to El Grande. I thought of crying instead, but that would be even worse.

"Are you afraid?" he asked, laughing.

"Sí, poco," I whimpered.

He laughed some more. "The bear is dead, *hombre.* I am sure."

"How do you know there is only one bear in there?" I asked with little hope that he would change his mind.

"Bears always sleep alone. They can't stand each other's snoring." He laughed so hard he almost rolled down to the horses.

I smiled weakly, just to be polite. I went down on my knees as if to pray, but instead I took the rope and crawled to the entrance. There I went down on my belly and began slithering like a snake into the dark and stinky cave. I slid deeper and deeper, but no bear. At the time I was about to throw up, I put my hand on a puddle of something. Whatever it was, I figured the bear had to be close. Finally I felt fur and long bony claws. I slipped the rope over them and headed for the light, kicking up so much dust I couldn't breathe.

For about another hour we pulled and dug and pulled some more. Finally the bulky mess slipped through the last part of the entrance. It was a bear! Shot twice through the neck.

By the time we dressed and loaded the bear on one of the horses it was nearly dark and snowing hard. We doubled up on the other horse and headed down the mountain. Long after dark we arrived back at the cabin, cold, hungry, and dead tired. Who would have guessed bear hunting was so much work?

While the bear hung in the cabin, dripping the last of its blood, we ate our food like starving coyotes. And as the powdery snow came down we went to sleep with our blood-stained clothes on. It was too cold to strip.

The next morning was so bright we could hardly see. Snow piled halfway up the door. We skinned and quartered the bear and hung the meat up in the attic. El Grande stretched the hide and carefully nailed it to the floor planks. Then we saddled up and headed back down the mountain. Later in the spring we would come back for the kill.

The whole *floresta* was buried in white and the trail was hidden. I was feeling good and I could tell El Grande was proud of me. Not everybody could say they had once crawled into a bear's den and roped one in the dark. In three hours we would be in the warm Capulín Cash Store with our feet up to the potbelly, telling stories about hunting bears in winter. Such thoughts made the time pass fast and we were soon at the bottom of the *cañoncito* headed toward the new road. As we came around the first little bend, we saw a dark-green truck parked in the middle of the road. Two men were standing as though they were waiting for somebody. Up close I could see the door of the truck had the head of a bear inside a circle. Below it said U.S. FOREST SERVICE.

"Hadidusa," El Grande said to the two *gringos.*

"Howdy," they both answered as they looked us over. "You fellas been up the mountain, have you?" one asked. El Grande turned and motioned for me to answer.

"Yes, sir," I said politely. One of them walked up to my horse, no doubt for a closer look.

"No les digas nada," El Grande mumbled under his breath.

"Mind if I ask what y'all were doing up there?"

"Dile que si ¿qué chinga'os le importa?" El Grande snorted. I was surprised to hear him cuss like that. For an instant I wondered how to translate.

"It's none of your damn business," I said as cold blood ran down my neck.

"Oh, I think it *is* our business. You see, I'm the new ranger around these parts," one of them said as he touched his hat. "I'd just like to know how both of you fellas got all that blood all over your clothes there." I looked down at my pants. El Grande did, too.

"¡PICALE A TU CABALLO!" El Grande screamed as he spurred his horse toward the man. The man stumbled back and fell. The other ran around the truck. My horse jumped. In a flash we were in a wild gallop down the road. Before the rangers turned around, we got to the shortcut trail and scooted down into the arroyo, up the other side and into the *piñón* forest. There was no way they could follow in their truck. We wove up and down arroyos until we finally came to a small mesa where we could see all around. El Grande got off his horse and doubled back to make sure we were not followed. I shivered.

"Qué rinches desgraciados," he said in a disgusted tone. I had not seen him so mad in a long time. We sat in the thicket until well after dark. Neither said much. I was sure we would go to prison. But then, would they put a kid like me in prison? I didn't want to be old enough to poach bears anymore. I felt the snow, fear, blood, cold, prison. For what? Rugs?

Under cover of the cold night, a million stars watching us, we sneaked down the back trail to the corral at the end of the *vega.* We quickly took the saddles off the horses and fed them. I think even the horses were scared because they didn't want to eat. From there we walked along the edge of the *monte* and down to the house. La Grande met us at the door.

"*¡Vagabundos!* Where have you been? I have been so worried."

"Ay, vieja mía. We just wanted to make our last bear hunt last a little longer," El Grande said as he put his big hand on her shoulder.

DIEZ

Who would ever think El Grande could stay in the house for days? He fixed doors that stuck and he cleaned the attic. He even painted the walls in La Grande's kitchen. He fed all the stock and did all his outside work at night. I knew why, but I didn't tell. Every morning I checked all the windows before I stepped out, too. You can't be too careful when you are a wanted man. For the rest of the winter I worked very hard in school to get the best grades, even better than the *gringo* kids. What *rinche* would want to put such a smart kid in prison? I thought. Even Mrs. Majors said that something wonderful must have come over me; that it must have sprinkled me with angel dust. Never did I confess that it was really bear blood.

In the Capulín Valley, when the smell of burning coal was gone, you knew it was spring. But this spring, when the wind was right, you also knew that the *molino* was very busy burning the scrap from the giant *floresta* trees that had been turned into boards. With the snow gone from the deep forest, the big logging trucks could get back to full time and everybody who wanted work had it. But not for the real men. The ones who were still ranch people didn't work for dollar pay.

They stayed with the land and they didn't have to worry about how much money they would have. El Grande said that they were still free. For them, it was time for the *acequia, el hijadero,* and the roundup.

We sat on the sunny side of the tool shed, la *resolana*, and he explained how the world works. El Grande was in one of his moods.

"Water, earth, and sun. They are all that life is. Of those, only water is for man to control," he said, pointing to the clouds with the fingers of his leathery hand. "Long ago the *indios* of the Chama and the Rio Grande were given the *acequia* by their wisdom. With it they moved the water from the river to their crops of *calabazas, maíz, frijol,* and *chile.* Then the sun shone on the earth and the plants grew. That is how the people lived and that is why the *acequia* is sacred." I listened quietly, but wondered if this story was a ploy to make me feel good about all the work that was about to start.

The *río del capulín* was born high in the *sierra* to the norte and tumbled through the *cañón del burro.* Winding its way through the deep forest, it finally came into the valley just above the *cuesta* where El Grande had found Mrs. Majors. The *acequia* took water from the Capulín Creek and ran along the high ground at the edge of the deep forest. Every spring the members all got together to clean out the big ditch. Some came to work, some to watch, many came to gossip, but everybody showed up. El Grande was always elected as the *mayordomo.* He called the meetings, set up the work crews, divided up the water and stopped all the fights. Before the *gringos* came, the *mayordomo* of the *acequia* and the priest were the most important people in the village.

Every year the *acequia* meeting happened around the potbelly at the store. This year there was a lot more *chisme* to catch up on: the *molino*, the *gringos,* the new *floresta* ranger, electricity, and no doubt a few little things about Mrs. Majors. There was talk about some *gringos* looking for oil up on the French Mesa, too. Rosa Velásquez had been dead for a long time, but the fireball she had turned into was still alive. And then there was the big one: The story about the bear hunt and how El Grande and his favorite grandson had to escape from the *pinches rinches*. Some even said it was not safe to hunt deer in the summertime anymore. Saturday was the day and nine o'clock was the time nobody would want to miss.

I was up early, to build a little fire to warm the place up some. A fire calms people's nerves, La Grande always said. Besides, the store had a lot of business lately, mostly *gringos* from the *molino*. My mother was happy. She had cleaned the place up until even the mice were wondering what was wrong. She wanted it to feel like a real business, not just the place where the *raza* came to spit and tell lies, she would say.

By the time I had the potbelly crackling, Tomas Casados was there, in his before-the-war Ford that blew so much smoke sometimes people thought it was on fire.

"Buenos días, Don Ezequiel," Tomas greeted as he stood up from where he had been warming his crotch. El Grande came in, carrying his trusty hex-barrel in his arms and his new hat on his head. Not only that, he had cut back his *pancho villa*, which meant he was ready for some big business! El Grande sat down in the only big chair in the store; everybody else took stools or the floor. Tomas said, *"Con permiso,"* as he reached into his pocket for his little sack of Bull Durham and paper. They always asked *permiso* to smoke when El Grande was around. In a little while Bernabé rolled up in his brand new Dodge Power Wagon, the only 4-wheel drive in the whole valley. It was red and pure macho. I dreamed that when I grew up I would have one, too. Right behind came Pedro, alone. Malvino had gone crazy again and had been sent back to the asylum.

Everybody sat around and talked and laughed for a long time. With every car that passed on the road the men would look to see who was coming. But nobody else came. I could tell El Grande was getting nervous, maybe even mad. Finally, close to ten, Tío Mateo and his sidekick, Perico, showed up.

Mateo was big. He always wore a large hat and red shirts. His Levi's stayed on with a wide belt and a huge silver belt buckle with turquoise chunks all over it. Everybody knew he had traded whisky to the Navajos for it. His black cowboy boots were always shiny and he wore spurs no matter what the work. He looked like the Gene Autry in the comics, except he was very brown. Perico was just Perico—short, fat, smelly, and always hungry. His big hook nose was why they called him Perico, parrot, no doubt.

Nobody else came. El Grande stood at the window with his gun propped next to him, and for a long time no one spoke. Where were all the others? It had never happened like this. Who would dare to miss the *acequia* meeting?

"Orden," he howled. He was mad. *"¿Dónde 'stán los otros?"* he asked, as if somebody had the answer. All the men shrugged and looked around as though looking for them. There was quiet for too long. Eyes settled down to just stare at the floor.

"Tal vez some of the men are working the shift at the *molino,"* Pedro said.

"I heard that Eduardo is sick, with a tooth gone bad," somebody else said. Every time anybody made a noise they all turned to look and hope, but no one else had any good ideas. El Grande looked at the floor as if it were a map to somewhere. Then he stood up.

"Everybody knows the rule: No work, no water." All of the men nodded. "The *acequia* will be dug next Saturday at eight. Bring tools. Shovels. Picks. Axes. And come strong. There is much work." He looked around, his eyes cold as ice. "If nobody has anything to say, that is all." El Grande put on his hat, picked up his rifle, and walked out the front of the Capulín Cash Store. Slowly, one by one, the men followed as if they were walking out of a funeral. Everybody, more or less, knew what had died.

El Grande was not the kind to quit when the going got hard. In the early afternoon we saddled up and headed up the red *caliche* highway to the outskirts of Capulín. Even the horses sensed his mood: Just do your job and shut up. I rode thinking that my main job was to just ride along and be quiet. Who knows what else would happen? I feared. When we reached Roberto's house, we yelled from the front. After more than a little while he came out.

"Buenas tardes, Don Ezequiel, *y tu tambien, chamaco,"* he said through his sleepy eyebrows. Then he said he was sorry. He was very tired from his job as a logger for the *molino* and couldn't come to the *acequia* meeting. But he said he knew that if you wanted water you had to help dig. "I don't know just yet if I will need water this year, but if I do, I will help," he said politely. Right away something told me he wasn't going to need water from the *acequia*. El Grande did his polite *despedida* and we rode on up the road.

Maclovio's house was next. "Yoo-hoo," El Grande leaned over in his saddle as though they could hear him better.

Tío Maclovio's daughter, Antonia, who was a little slow, opened the door and asked who it was, as if she couldn't see us. El Grande asked for Maclovio. She just shut the door with no word. After a little while she opened it again and said that her father was very sick. El Grande leaned back in his saddle, pushed his hat to the back of his head, and mumbled something about a tooth.

We rode on. As the day was coming to a tired end it sounded like the jobs at the *molino* were very hard and there was a lot of sickness all over Capulín, bad teeth and worse. The only good excuse came from Torpe Molina, the father of the ape kid. He appeared at the door, two black eyes, a cut on the mouth, and a red rag tied around his head. He said he had been in a fight with some *gringos* at the Capulín Bar the night before. He wasn't sure who had won. But fight or no fight, he was going to help.

With no more left to visit we rode back toward the village, the sun already headed straight down to the Apache nation of the Jicarilla past the French Mesa. El Grande muttered something every once in a while, but I couldn't make it out and I didn't dare ask. He was mad. I could tell because he sat very straight in the saddle—as he did when he was angry. When we finally got back to the house, we watered and fed the horses. I couldn't stand the quiet.

"What are you thinking, Grande?" I finally asked, hoping that he wouldn't explode.

"This year we are going to have all the water from the *acequia* that we need," he said with a little nod. Then he turned and looked right at me. "Maybe even enough water to take a bath every day!" He laughed all the way down to his belly. He was getting over his ugly mood.

On Monday I was again one of Mrs. Majors' pupils. The school year would end soon and we were behind in everything, she kept saying. Double arithmetic homework was the worst. Who would ever want to spend his whole life looking at numbers? Besides all the arithmetic, I had been sentenced to no recess ever since the fight with the Tusa. Only good thing was that he was in there, too. At first we would kick or pinch when Mrs. Majors wasn't watching. He would call me dumb Mexican kid and I would call him smelly *gringo pendejo.* But after a while we figured we might as well be friends for at least a half-hour a day. Nobody would know. We even helped one another with the arithmetic.

El Grande didn't do arithmetic; he did real work. All week he worked in the tool shed getting picks, shovels, axes, and everything else we would need on Saturday for the big dig. Everyone was supposed to bring his own tools, but El Grande brought extras to erase all the excuses.

Saturday morning, at the cut-off gate from the *Río Capulín,* the first business was to see who finally showed up. *"Del dicho al hecho hay mucho trecho,"* El Grande always said. Ricardo and José came first, then Pedro. Tomas Casados showed and after him Perico, who said that Mateo wasn't coming because he was sick. Two others came shortly after and the last one to show up, at eight-thirty, was Lorenzo, the ape kid. He said his father wasn't coming, no excuse.

El Grande called everybody together. He said we would dig as far as Tomas's land, the last *ranchito* of the ones who came to work. He divided us into two teams: José, Tomas, Ricardo, the ape kid, and me on one team. The rest on the other. He told my team to count a thousand paces twice along the ditch, then to work back upstream to the one-thousand mark. The other team would work down to the same mark. Whoever got there first won. Then we would do it again to see which team won the most times. It was just like the World Series that my father listened to on the radio. This was the world series of ditch digging.

With shovels and picks in hand, we paced down the ditch, made a mark at a thousand paces, and kept going to two. There we elected Tomas our *capitán* and named ourselves the Diesel Macks, in honor of the big trucks that hauled the huge loads of logs to the *molino*. Since the other team was mostly the old men, we named them *Burros Viejos*.

A blast from El Grande's trusty hex-barrel and the digging started. The Diesel Macks tossed dirt, cut roots, and stacked rocks like yellow machines. Tomas watched that we did everything right and we did everything our *capitan* said. The first round was no problem; we dusted them by a hundred paces. The old men looked at our sweaty faces and patted us on the back. "What men these young ones are," they said with their eyes. We believed it and by the end of the second round, we had won twice.

At noon we all sat under a big pine and ate our *lonche*. All the talk was about who was going to win. We didn't even want to stop to eat. Before time was up we paced off and yelled for the signal. When the blast came we worked even faster. We were now a real team and the digging got easier downstream. By late afternoon we were down to the last thousand paces and the *Burros* had no points. Somebody said we should let them win one. "*¡Chale!*" everybody else yelled. So finally, at the end of the day, the teams met at the *compuerta* where Tomas would get his water. The score: Diesel Macks 5, *Burros Viejos—nada!* The old men looked at one another with little smiles, no doubt wanting to feel good even if they lost.

From where we were all standing at the edge of the deep forest we could see the whole valley. The *molino* was in front of the French Mesa, with the scrap burner sending a cloud of white smoke high into the sky. We could hear the growl of a chain saw from somewhere below. Up high, a flock of geese was honking north.

We had done the work of many men. Laughing, talking, cleaning tools, we were all sweaty and hungry. Proud, too. The *acequia* was ready.

Off alone, El Grande stood quiet, water in his eyes.

The *acequia* was just the beginning of springtime work. Stuck between Mrs. Majors and El Grande, my life bounced between dividing fractions and the growing chores of the rancho. It was a time when all the fun of the fall turned into the sticky mess of being born. Everything was having babies: Cows, sheep, goats, chickens, and even the women from the *molino.* Some came into the store with these little pink people wrapped in white blankets. They bought them Pet Milk and some kind of cereal my mother had ordered just for them. Even Torpe Molina came to the store with a magazine opened to a page that said you could order three hundred chicks for ten dollars. He asked my mother to fill in the form, since he didn't know how to write. She tried to tell him that three hundred little mouths would get to be a lot of big mouths to feed. She was a practical woman. But no matter. He said he would just turn them loose along the *acequia*—plenty of food and drink. His job would be to watch where they laid the eggs.

El Grande had the hardest job. In the cold nights of the early spring a newborn calf or lamb could freeze. And there were always plenty of hawks, eagles, and coyotes looking around for an easy lunch. He had to watch them all. But the stickiest job came when a calf was being born feet first. I never understood why, but it was bad. El Grande had to set up his net, ropes, and tools to tie up the mother and dig out the baby. To me it was a miracle from God that he was able to keep them alive without throwing up.

The last big job of the spring was the roundup. Just like the *acequia,* all the men had to come and help. Every young calf had to be branded, ears cut, and shoulder shot for the black leg disease. The boy calves also had to have their little *cositas* cut off.

This year, just as always, El Grande let everybody know when it was going to happen. All week he was busy getting his branding irons ready, his knives honed, and the *vacuna* needles sharpened like fish hooks.

For me, it was still school, Mrs. Majors, and double the work. The Tusa had become a good friend, maybe because we had been together for so long in Mrs. Majors' jail. I even invited him to the roundup. He was very excited and all week he ran around the schoolyard acting like a cowboy. What does he know about cows? I wondered.

The great Saturday of the roundup finally came. By the time I was out the door and headed down the little trail to the big corral, El Grande already had four horses saddled and the fire for the irons blazing orange. The smell of burning *piñón,* the song of a million birds and the yellow *vega* of dandelions all made me feel like working. In the distance I could see *tío* Mateo and Perico riding down the hill, and way back on the dirt road I could see a kid running. I was sure it was the Tusa. When I got to the horses, I jumped on one and galloped out to meet Mateo and Perico. Mateo was in his leather chaps, silver spurs, black gloves, and big, big hat. In the light of the rising sun, all the silver on his clothes and his saddle glittered like lightning on top of his *palomino*. As I rode up he roped me with his braided leather rope, the one and only in the valley. I wiggled to get loose and he laughed. After the quick, *"Buenos días,"* I rode on to meet the Tusa. He was full of cheer. I hoisted him up on the horse and we rode back to the fire. El Grande was all business.

"*¿Y tú, cómo te llamas, amigo?*" he asked the Tusa. The kid's eyes stopped on me, as though asking for help.

"He wants to know what your name is," I said.

"Oh, my name is Alvin, sir." He smiled. "But they call me Tusa at school ... and sometimes *pendéjo!*" El Grande tried not to laugh, I could tell.

"Tusa. *Tú eres buen hombre.* You, *lumbre.*" El Grande pointed to the hot flames.

"You're in charge of the fire, *pendéjo,*" I kidded him. "He likes you."

We knew what to do. Mateo, Perico, and I galloped off into the *vega* to drive the first part of the herd into the corral, twenty or thirty at a time. The cows really didn't want to break down into groups, but with good horses they soon found out they had to obey. By the time we got back with the first bunch, Tomas had arrived, but no one else. Just like the *acequia,* it was going to be a long day.

To say we worked hard would not be correct. We worked harder than just hard. Perico and Mateo on the ropes, Tomas knocking them down, El Grande with the irons and the knife, and me with the *vacuna;* I liked being the doctor. Tusa was the fire man. One by one—the smell of burning hide, the blood and the cries of pain. Who would want to put so many babies through all of this? I wondered. Rancho life was a little sad.

What had started as a beautiful spring day finally ended long, bloody, smelly, sweaty, and full of bruises. The *marcadero* was finished and so were we. But what came next was the best *comida* that La Grande fixed all year: Meat, potatoes, *chile,* beans, rice and a very tall stack of tortillas. In honor of the boy calves it was tradition to have some fine, deep-fried "mountain oysters." They tasted good, too! Then after a little rest came apple pie, sweet cream, and chokecherry syrup. What dusty cowboy would want to quit and die now?

"I never ate at a Mexican house before. What do I do?" the Tusa asked as we all sat down at the table, steaming food everywhere.

"You just eat, *pendéjo!*" I punched him on the arm to calm him down a little. He looked over the table, trying to find peanut butter or mustard, no doubt.

El Grande said grace. He thanked God for the herd and the success of the day; for all the helpers who had come, especialmente for the Tusa; and for the food. Then everybody passed the food around, fast.

"How did you like those little crispy meats?" I asked the Tusa, pointing to the tradition of the day.

"I like them, but what are they?" Everybody waited for me to tell him.

"¡No le digas! De malas se muere si sabe," El Grande said, laughing. *"Ahora sí eres puro vaquero,"* he added, looking at the Tusa with pride.

"Don't even worry what they are. He says that now you are a real cowboy. And if he says so, it's true," I explained.

Many days later El Grande and I sat on the porch of the Capulín Cash Store. I had been wondering if it was all right that the Tusa had come to the roundup. I had never asked permission.

"Yes. It has to be all right," he said. "But you must learn their ways the same way he has started to learn ours. Learn how they think. Learn to be like they are. Like the *camaleón* that changes colors to survive. But just as the *camaleón* never forgets that he is a lizard, you must never forget who you are. You must be proud of who you are." I imagined myself as a lizard of many colors, turning the color of the ground, the rocks and the trees, going everywhere the *gringos* were, but never seen. I would know their secrets. I would live two lives, maybe more.

"Soon all that will be left of the old ways will be what is in your head and in your soul. You must protect the treasure."

ONCE

El Grande was right. The *gringos* kept coming. Every few days a new family rolled past the store and on to the community of the *molino*. The kids came to school, the mamas to the store and the papas to the Capulín Bar.

Before the *gringos,* the bar was just a long room with two windows, a door, and a step made of rocks. A little sign painted on the wall above the door was proud to say CAPULIN BAR, and on either side of the door were round metal ones for "Pabst Blue Ribbon" beer. When the *gringos* came, a new porch made of thick *molino* boards was added to make it look fancy. More signs, too; for Camels, Luckys, and even one with an almost naked woman and a bottle of whiskey. Even more important, another outhouse was made. They said it was for the women. On the uphill side of the bar was the icehouse. Before the R.E.A. came to Capulín, big blocks of ice were cut from the frozen dams and stored under tons of sand in the icehouse for the hot days of summer. On some Saturday afternoons, sweating all over, we got to smash ice blocks into chunks and load the icebox in the bar. If the man wasn't looking we would steal a bottle of beer and hide it in the icehouse. Later, ten or more young men of Capulín would sneak off to the deep arroyo and get drunk on one stolen ice-cold beer. So by the time the old men who were able to get loose started showing up at the Capulín Bar for the Saturday night peda, we had already had our turn!

Inside the bar, it smelled like rotting barley. Along one side was the bar with steel stools nailed to the plank floor. A pool table was in the middle of the room, with a few chairs scattered around. At one time the walls had been painted pink. Now they were mostly brown. The jukebox was behind the bar, protected from flying things. Without the Mexican music it made, the bar would be just a noisy whiskey store.

The guys and I were not allowed inside, but we could sit on the porch and look when El Grande wasn't watching from across the river. Saturday night was best. The ones who worked for money got paid. The ones who didn't have any money just came to be friendly, but it wasn't long before almost everybody was drunk. In Capulín, if you had money you bought until it was gone. Women hardly ever came, except a few from other villages, and they didn't stay long. They were soon taken away by the men to do things we were not supposed to know about.

The Apaches of the Jicarilla came, too. It was rumored that they were not supposed to drink by law, but nobody had tried to find out for sure. They never had money, but they had rugs they got from the Navajo. Somebody always needed another saddle blanket or a rug for the cold floor of winter. Besides, as the night went on, a saddle blanket for a beer was a good trade.

There was no Indian like El Mocho. He was big, his long hair tied with a red rag around his square head; and his Levi's were unbuttoned at the top to let his belly hang out a little more. His voice was like thunder and he played the guitar so good even though his right hand was missing. A horse had ripped it off at the wrist, they said. He strapped a big "thumb" of wood to the stump of his arm and his music made all the drunks want to cry about love. The Indians all spoke Spanish, so everybody understood the music. They were almost like everyone else, except they knew more languages and they lived in the *reserva.*

As the *molino* grew, *gringos* started coming to the bar. In the early days they just got beer and took it home. But now they came in little groups and stayed to drink. Some of the men who worked at the *molino* knew and talked to them. Others made little jokes about them. Some said they were stingy. Others said they smelled funny. The *gringos* all had money and they always sat together, but they never bought a beer for anybody.

Torpe Molina hated them, and he told them. *"Pinches gabachos,"* he would say as he stumbled out to the porch where we were. Nobody minded him much. They all knew how he was; a little bit loco. They said he had gone crazy when his wife ran off to California with a stranger. The only thing he did right was raise chickens. Lots of them. He had so many that they ran wild all over the valley, leaving nests full of eggs everywhere. People gathered them just like wild spinach or chokecherries. They said no one in Capulín would ever starve because they could always hunt for Torpe's eggs. Everybody made jokes about, *"los huevos de Torpe!"*

I slept where I got sleepy, at El Grande's or at home. It made no difference. That particular Saturday night I had stayed across the road because La Grande had made *menudo.* Who would miss such a thing? Early that Sunday morning, coming out of some confused dream, I heard a stiff rap at the door. I jumped out of bed and ran to see who it was before El Grande had a chance to come from the other end of the house. It was Bernabé, standing on the porch with his hat in his hand. He had a worried look.

"Buenos días, muchacho. ¿Está Don Ezequiel?" he asked. He stood a bit more stiffly when El Grande came to the door. "Don Ezequiel, please pardon me for being here at your door so early on Sunday, but we have what is probably a very seri-

ous problem in the community," he said with sadness in his voice.

"*¿Pues, qué pasa, hombre?*" El Grande asked.

"Early this morning Maclovio found a man under the bridge—a dead man. A gringo."

"*¡Madre Santa! Que Dios lo tenga en la gloria,*" El Grande said, automatically making the sign of the cross even though he wasn't Catholic. I guess in such times you grab whatever religion gets to you first. Then he turned to keep me from hearing what I had just heard. I stood there stunned. All my blood drained down to my feet. I thought I might faint.

Before I could even think about getting into my clothes, El Grande and Bernabé were getting into the Dodge Power Wagon. El Grande had his hex-barrel in his arms. I watched them drive down the road; then I ran across to tell the terrible news, still wearing nothing but my *chones*.

My father, home for the weekend from his teaching job at Coyote, got dressed and ran to the bridge. He didn't let me go. Instead, my mother and I watched from the porch. A group of men was already there, some on the bridge, some under. Maybe it is the *abuelo* they found, I thought. After all, it was his hiding place.

For a long time we just looked and waited. I could barely keep from running down there, even though a visit with the leather *reata* would be a sure thing. Finally! Two in front and two in back, some men carried something in a canvas up the steep slope and put it into Bernabé's truck. "It's the body," my mother whispered and prayed. My heart started jumping when I saw them turning around to head back toward the store.

The last dead person I had seen was Rosa Velásquez, but she was one of us and she was a witch. A dead *gringo* had to be special. I wondered if he would look different, or whether we looked all the same when dead. I was going to see him even if I had to disobey.

The truck rolled up the road, pulled into the drive, and up in front of the gas pump. Some of the men were riding with the body while others walked. My mother held my shoulder for a moment, but I got loose and ran to the truck to look. The body was lying face up covered only from the waist down. The man's arm was sticking up as though he were waving good-bye and his mouth was open with dirt in it. His shirt was splattered with blood that had turned black and his face was white like paper. I felt like throwing up.

El Grande came around the truck and asked my mother for a sheet. He opened the tailgate, climbed up, and squatted next to the body. When the sheet came he took the canvas off, spread out the sheet, and asked two men to lift the man onto the middle. Then he put his weight on the man's arm to bend it down to his side. It made some crackling noises. Everybody looked to see if it would come back up. It didn't. El Grande carefully wrapped the body in the sheet, tied the loose ends, and finished the job as if it were a chore he did almost every day.

Now what? Everybody looked around. El Grande was in deep thought. Suddenly my father said that they should have an inquest. Somebody asked what that was. Somebody else said they should just take the body to the county seat at Tierra Amarilla. Bernabé said that he thought somebody had gone to Coyote to call the law.

While the men were figuring what to do next, a truck with four *gringos* came down the road and stopped. One leaned out the window and yelled, "Y'all seen ma brother Luke 'round here anywheres?" No answer. "Last time we seen him wuz last night ouch yonder at the bar." He waited. Still no answer. "He 'n that Molina feller stepped outside to have a few words." A few feet got shuffled and some throats got cleared.

"¿Qué dice ese hombre?" El Grande finally asked. He looked at my father. He didn't answer, but he took a few steps to the back of the truck with the body.

"You better come and look over here," he said to the men as he pointed to the white bundle. I could tell he was scared. The *gringos* jumped out of their truck and ran to Bernabé's truck. The first one there untied the neat wrap and peeled back the sheet.

"Holy Jesus Christ, it's Luke!" he whimpered. "He's dead, he's dead, he's dead," he cried. The others just stared at the dead man's face. "Ma brother is dead here." He covered his face with his hands for a moment. Then he pulled a red handkerchief from his back pocket and blew his nose hard. "Who done it?" he yelled. "Who done it, goddamnit!" he yelled even louder.

"Todavía no sabemos," El Grande said in his official voice.

"We don't know yet," my father repeated.

"I know who done it," the man who was crying yelled. "It was that goddamn, sonnovabitch Molina. I want to know where he lives so I can go kill the little bastard." At that moment El Grande walked around Bernabé's truck and picked up his rifle.

"Orden. Orden," he commanded. "Until the county sheriff gets here or we have an inquest and take this dead man to Tierra Amarilla, I am the law here." The *gringos* looked at him wondering what he had said. Nobody moved. El Grande was in charge.

Suddenly one of the *gringos* jumped and slapped the rifle away from El Grande and tossed it over to one of his friends. "You ain't the law 'round here, ole man. You're likely ta kill somebody else wid'at piece of junk," the *gringo* said angrily. Another *gringo* ran to their truck and brought out two pistols.

"Now, who's goin'ta show us where that Molina lives?" he asked, eyes back and forth. No one blinked. "How 'bout you, ole man?"

"Diles que todos están arrestados," El Grande hollered to my father.

"He says you are all under arrest," my father said. "He is the recognized law here in Capulín, but he doesn't speak English," he explained.

"Sheat! We're the ones with the guns here. One of you meskins is goin'ta take us to Molina so as we can do to that greaser what he done to Luke," the man with the two pistols shouted. He walked around the group of men, keeping an eye on everybody, with both pistols pointed at them. When he got to the porch, he stopped. "How 'bout you, kid? You know where Molina lives, don't you?" he asked me as I stood near my mother.

"Yes sir, I do," I answered politely.

"Aw right. You lead the way, boy," he ordered. My mother took a step, grabbed me by the neck and said no. "Don't worry, lady. When he points to Molina's house, I'll cut him loose." All I heard was, "cut him." I was shivering. As I started moving I looked over at El Grande, sure that he was going to do something. He would not let them go off with his rifle. And what about me? He would jump them or something. I walked with the gringos, two of them, past the body, past El Grande, and started around their truck. Nobody moved. They all stood stiffly, with their arms crossed over their bellies. It began to sink in that I was in danger of taking the *gringos* across the *vega* and the oak thickets and getting Torpe killed. I figured I would go slow. El Grande needed more time to figure it all out. Even if Torpe was about worthless, El Grande would save him anyway. I started to cross the road with the *gringos,* but lucky for me a car came around the curve by the *monte,* really fast. We could make it, but why hurry! As the car came close I heard somebody yell, "*¡Es la ley!* The *chota* is coming!"

The car slid to a stop, almost sideways on the dirt road. When the dust cleared, I could read the words on the shiny black door: STATE POLICE. I could have kissed the dirt road with wet lips. Hardly ever did we see the *chota*. What for? El Grande kept the peace. But here he was, just in time, and in his slick black suit with shiny buttons and a star over his heart. His gun was big—one of those *mata-gigantes*.

The *chota* jumped out of the car and headed straight toward me and the *gringo* with the two pistols. "Gimme de guns," he ordered. "Stend over here against de car." He meant business. He lined up all the *gringos,* hands up against the police car. He told me to get out of the way. Then he searched them all. El Grande now stepped forward.

"Buenos días, Naranjo,"

"Ah, buenos días, Don Ezequiel," the *chota* answered, and reached to shake El Grande's hand. It was the famous Ermiñio Naranjo, about whom El Grande had told many stories. Once, he had even helped him catch some cow thieves. *"¿Pues, qué pasa aquí?"* the *chota* asked. El Grande grumbled something as he walked over and picked up his rifle where the chota had piled up the guns. Then he walked over to the car, grabbed the *gringo* that had slapped his rifle away and turned him around. He stuck the barrel in the *gringo's* belly and stared at him. Everybody stood shocked. "Oh, God," somebody in the crowd whimpered.

"Gringo baboso," El Grande growled in a low voice. Even the *chota* was surprised.

"¡No! ¡No! Eso no, Don Ezequiel," the *chota* said as he ran to the car. El Grande turned and walked over to the crowd of people and stood again with his rifle in his arms. He was trembling. I had never seen him so mad in all my life.

The lawman slowly put the facts together. He took three men, Maclovio, Bernabé and one of the *gringos*, and went looking for Torpe. He told El Grande to guard the other *gringos*, even the dead one. My father was sent to the bridge to keep people away. The rest of us watched from the porch.

The news spread fast. People came to the store instead of going to Mass. With nobody in the church, the priest came, too. He even blessed the dead man. The people made the sign of the cross and prayed for the dead stranger. When they talked they whispered, and even though they waited a long time for something else to happen, nobody got rowdy. Those who got hungry went into the store and got candy and Coca-Cola and left the money on the counter. Who would want to be dishonest at a time like this?

It was almost noon when the *chota* and the others showed up with Torpe. By now many people from the *molino* were there. Torpe looked very happy, saying good morning to everybody and smiling all over. The *chota* took him over to the car and sat him in the back seat. He told Bernabé and Maclovio to guard him while he went to the bridge. A long line of people followed the *chota* down the road. Not since the Virgin de Guadalupe had been taken on her yearly outing had there been such a procession. The *chota* looked all around, picked up pieces of stuff he found and put them in a bag. He drew a picture of the scene and put it in his shirt pocket. Then he walked back up the road, all the people following again. When he had packed all his things in the trunk of the car he took Torpe over to the body.

"Do you re-conice dis man?" he asked in English.

"Chure I do. *Es* dat *hijo de la chingada* Luke. Lo *maté* por *cabrón."* A sigh from the crowd followed. Torpe had just admitted he had killed the *gringo* in front of everybody.

"You're going to burn in hell for this, you bastard," one of the *gringo* women yelled from the crowd. With that, Torpe leaned over and spit on the dead man's face. Then he looked up and smiled, his rusty-brown teeth all in a row. He was a happy man. Nobody had ever seen Torpe quite like this before.

It was late in the afternoon when the chota finally finished asking questions. Even I was asked if I had heard anything that night. When was the last time I saw Torpe? Had I ever seen Torpe and the *gringo* fight before? Wasn't I one of the kids who hung around the bar? I was proud to be asked and I told the truth, too. The only thing I knew was that Luke and Torpe had argued once on the porch of the bar and Luke had called him a greaser or something like that.

The *chota* put Torpe in the back seat of the car and chained his hands and feet to the floor. He shook El Grande's hand and drove away. Bernabé and Maclovio followed with the body. The *gringos* were crying and hugging each other. Some of the people of Capulín cried, too. Everybody asked questions that had no answers. Nobody seemed to want to leave.

Suddenly the voice of a boy came from across the road. *"Papacito, Papacito,"* he cried. It was Lorenzo, the ape kid. He wanted his father. He asked where he was but no one answered. They just stared at the ground. Then slowly El Grande walked toward him and put his hand on his shoulder. He whispered something to him and led him toward his house.

DOCE

The killing of Luke Evans shook the valley. All people talked about was the murder. Who would have ever believed it could happen in Capulín? And poor Torpe. There he was in Tierra Amarilla, in jail, while his chickens got even more wild. What will the *gringos* think? That we are not good people, or what?

Then there was Lorenzo, the ape kid—he had lived with El Grande until they were able to find his mother in a place called Fresno. I was happy they found her. Sure, I felt sorry for the ape kid, but he was taking up too much with El Grande. I think he was even starting to like him. Besides, it was Fresno's turn to have an ape kid.

The *molino* got bigger and bigger and more men from the village went to work for the Duke City. Some got to be loggers in the forest and others worked at the mill. All day and all night, the round saws ate up the trees from the deep forest. The scrap burner turned what was left after they made boards into black smoke and the smell of burning pine was all over. Some days you thought the sun was getting weak. My mother cursed the dust and the soot and the noise and the lack of business. The *gringos* hardly ever went to the bar or came to the store anymore. They got their things from the big city, and not even my mother's bargains got them to stop in. Those *gringos* are not so smart shoppers, she took to saying.

At school Torpe was a bandit. The *gringo* kids said he was. Mrs. Majors used him to teach how lazy people get to be drunks and finally murderers. He was supposed to be a lesson for all of us so that we would never turn out to be like him. She said we, thank God, would all turn out to be good, English-speaking citizens.

Some of us were confused. Torpe had been so brave and fearless when the *chota* had him under arrest. He had smiled and waved to everybody. He even spit on the dead man. Who would be so happy on his way to jail except a man with lots of *huevos*? we thought. But if Mrs. Majors said he was a bad man, he was a bad man. The teacher was always right.

El Grande was working hard with his spring chores. What's worse, he seemed to be very different. It had become hard to talk to him because he was always in his mood. The first job of spring in the upper rancho was to check the fences and fix the water holes. In past years Torpe and other men had gone up to help him, but now there was nobody. Everybody was doing something else, so El Grande had gone to the upper rancho alone and three weeks with no word was too long for La Grande. She asked my mother to help her decide what to do, which she hardly ever did.

The road to the upper rancho at La Mesa had been finished by the Duke City so that now you could drive a truck to about a mile from the cabin, maybe two. The rest of the way was mud and rocks and only good for El Grande's team of horses. Then there was always walking.

In the early morning of a sunny day my mother and La Grande drove me to the top of the mountain. I rode in the back with two of the dogs just for company and fresh air. Along the way we met big logging trucks loaded with what used to be pine trees, but now were logs headed for the teeth of the round saws. My mother was afraid and she almost went in the side ditch to let them pass. *"Trocas malditas,"* she would yell. The dogs barked ferociously, but I just waved and yelled, "Hey, toot your horn!" I liked the blast of their air horns.

At the top of the mountain they let me off and told me to start walking. I was to find El Grande at the cabin and tell him to come home the next day. They would pick us up at the same spot at sunset. La Grande needed him for who knows what. I think she was just lonely.

I knew the mountain. Every summer since I was five or six I had come to the mesa to help with the chores of the rancho. Walking down the little valley, to the left were the tall cliffs where eagles nested. To the right were the aspen slopes where the wild turkeys liked to hide the most. Down the middle was the little stream that, by the end of summer, was almost dry. I first came to the *potrero,* and beyond it was the big potato patch where El Grande raised all the *papitas* Capulín could ever eat. Then came the *vega* from where I could first see the cabin, sitting on a little hump on the left of the valley. I stopped to rest at a spot where I could see all around. Far to the *norte* I could see the snow-covered San Juan mountains, which El Grande said were really in Colorado. In between them and me was the Mesa De Las Viejas, flat as a *molino* board. Below it, the Chama River. To the right of it was the Cerro Del Pedernal, looking just like a funnel turned upside down. El Grande told many stories about it, too. He said that in the old days Indians from all over came there to gather the flint from which they made arrow points, and to trade. That was the only place in the world where all the tribes that were enemies came in peace. It was a sacred place.

All around me, little flowers were poking their white, pink, and blue faces out of the wet ground. Birds were chirping everywhere. The blue jays were the worst; they seemed to fight about everything. Along the edge of the forest, the *sombrillo,* snowbanks were still hanging on. Up high, hawks made slow, lazy circles in the blue sky. I lay back on the big rock. Who could ever worry about fractions or murders or *molino* noise in a place like this? Someday I would own this whole mountain, with hundreds of cows on it. My horses would all be *palominos.* I would grow more potatoes than El Grande and kill two bears every year. I would have lots of guns and even a wife; maybe a *gringa* like Susie Kimball. She would cook big pots of beans and *chile* for me and my men. We would all burp and nobody would dare to tell us it wasn't polite. I touched myself down there and it felt good.

I had spent more time resting than I was supposed to. The sun was already high in the sky as I ran along the trail, slapping all the trees I passed along the way. I saw fences that were still down and wondered if El Grande had seen them yet. Springs leaking water, too. Puffing hard, I finally climbed the little hill up to the wooden gate of the *jardin* near the cabin. I had seen no sign of El Grande so I was sure he was in the cabin, probably fixing something. I thought I would yell for him but I changed my mind. Instead I thought I would pretend I was a lion, sneak inside and jump him when I got inside. The little trail came around the back of the cabin and up to the side of the porch. Running fast, I turned the corner, jumped the steps to the porch and crashed into something hanging. I looked. *¡MADRE SANTA!* BONES! It was a skeleton: a skull, ribs, arms and legs, no feet, as though they had been eaten away by the coyotes or something. It had been a person. It only had a few teeth left, but I thought I recognized them.

"¡GRANDE!" I screamed. *GRANDE—Grande—grande,* the echo came back from the side of the mountain. I covered my eyes to blind me from this terrible thing. Then I looked again. Is it...

"¡OYES, HOMBRE!" The thunder voice came from somewhere down the hill near the spring. I turned. There he was, working his way up the trail with a big bucket in each hand and a smile all the way across his face. *"¿Qué hay de nuevo,*

hijo?" he asked as he came up close. I rubbed my eyes and looked again. It really was him, but I didn't answer. I just stood frozen on the porch, with the skeleton. "Well, can't you talk? It is good to see you. And my friend there is happy to see you, too, but you should at least say good morning, *muchacho.* It is not polite." He belly, laughed as he put the buckets of water down.

"I thought it was you... hanging there," I muttered. He gave another big laugh.

"No, *hombre,* I couldn't be that ugly! Look. No feet, even," he said as he climbed the two steps up to the porch. He put his hand on the skull and turned it like it was supposed to talk to me. "For over two hundred years she has been lying deep in the ground wondering what is going on. She and the rest of her tribe owned all this land before me, all of it, and they took good care of it, too. I decided to dig her up so she could see what is happening." Then he turned her face toward the aspen forest. "Her name is Antigua. I want her to hang here so she can help me keep a close watch over the mountain. Maybe she can keep it from being destroyed." My pounding heart was slowing down and I sat on the side of the porch to rest. He was in a very strange mood, as if he had gone a little wild.

"How come you haven't fixed all the fences yet?" I asked. "I saw some parts that are still down. Have you been sick or what?"

"Sick? No, I have been working very hard. Besides helping Antigua get herself put back together, I have been getting ready for the big famine. Come in, you will see." He led the way into the cabin.

On the kitchen floor were two dead deer. On the table were pans of meat. A deer hide was hanging from the *vigas* at one end of the room. The place smelled awful. He asked me to look in the attic. I climbed the stairs and found four wires strung the length of the cabin filled with jerky. More hides, too. "What a killing," I said as I came back down the skinny stairs.

"A good hunter will never go hungry," he bragged. He went into the bedroom part of the cabin and brought out a bow and a fistful of arrows. "This is how I did it. Like the ancients. The bow is made of *palo duro*. And look at these arrows; they have fine points of flint. I chipped them myself. This is what Antigua's people used. It is the best weapon a man can hunt with. It is deadly. It is quiet. It doesn't cost any money. It is a little gift from the mountain." He looked at his bow as though he wanted to kiss it. "I want to show you where Antigua comes from. I think this afternoon we will pack a little camp and spend the night out there," he added.

I was tired, but who would want to argue? He sounded like he wouldn't hear me say no, anyway.

In one sack we packed some food: jerky, potatoes, and bread. Also a pan, forks, and spoons. Blankets and a small tarp in another. He also carried his bow and arrows. I carried a small shovel. In the early afternoon we headed down the valley and along the edge of the forest to a point where we picked up a trail to a ridge he called *La Mesita*. Right away it brought memories of dead bears. We had crossed the same place on our way to the bear dens. The forest had looked very different in winter. Now there was tender grass everywhere and the leaves of the aspens were starting to sprout. Birds, rabbits, and the noisy tree squirrels were all around. The breeze was at least warm.

El Grande always walked fast and it was hard keeping up with him even though he was carrying the heaviest load. In late afternoon we arrived at the Indian ruins. All that was left from a long time ago was a short piece of a rock wall and lots of other rocks scattered all around, but he said this had been a big Indian camp. He acted as though he had visited them. Nearby there was a bowl-shaped sink in the ground and in the middle, the grave where he had dug up the skeleton. We built a lean-to with the tarp and dug a fire pit lined with flat rocks. While El Grande dug around the ruins, I gathered firewood. I wondered what it had been like to be an Indian—no school, no barbed-wire fence to fix and no trucks.

By the time it got dark, El Grande had fixed a tasty meal which we ate out of the same pan. He ate slow to let me get my share. He said that everything we were eating had come from the mountain—no machines, no electricity, and no guns to get it. He said that the best education was to know the forest and to understand the animals. There was food all around us. Even parts of the pine trees were good. There was *pedernal* to make arrow points and axes. Fire could be made by turning a special kind of stick back and forth in your hands. When I said it was better to just use matches, he got mad.

We sat around the fire not saying much. The sky had a million stars and they all looked closer than ever. The cool breeze swept the tall forest and it sounded like a river. I stared at the dancing flames and wondered what fire really really was. Antigua and her people must have sat at the same place long ago and wondered the same thing. A shooting star streaked across the sky and on behind the trees. It brought Rosa Velásquez to my mind. I thought about Mrs. Majors and school and how much things had changed. And the murder was no small thing. I was about to fall asleep when I saw El Grande pull something like a book from his pocket. It was a Bible. That was really strange!

"In the Lord I take refuge.
How can you say to me: Flee
like a bird to your mountain.
For look, the wicked bend their
bows: They set their arrows
against the strings to shoot
from the shadows at the upright
in heart."

He stopped reading and wiped his eyes with his hand—tears flowed down his face. Strain from the dim light, no doubt. He went on reading, some out loud and some to himself.

"How long, O Lord? Will you
forget me forever? How long will
you hide your face from me?
How long must I wrestle with
my thoughts and every day have
sorrow in my heart?
Give light to my eyes, or I will
sleep in death."

I wanted to ask him why he was reading such awful stuff, but what if he gave me a more awful answer? He had never done any of this. It was at a point where I was getting a little scared, but thanks to God he finally put his Bible down. I asked him if he was sleepy. He didn't answer. He just stared at the fire and hummed a little tune, the same one I had heard before. I tried to act like nothing was wrong and told him I was going to sleep. I picked up a blanket, wrapped myself in it and laid down in the lean-to.

Cuatro milpas tan solo que han quedado
de aquel ranchito que era mío,
de aquella casita, tan blanca y bonita,
lo triste que está.
Los potreros están sin ganado,
todito se acabó.

TRANSLATION OF "CUATRO MILPAS
[Four planted fields, oh how abandoned they are now,
From that little farm that once was mine,
From that little house, so white and fine.
Oh how sad it all is now.
The grazing fields are now without horses,
Everything has come to an end.]

He put words to his little tune for the first time that I could remember. I peeked out at him from inside the blanket and saw more strain from the dim light shining in his eyes. I knew that whatever was happening in his mind was bad for him; and if it was bad for him, it was bad for me, too. I cried under the blanket, quiet. I prayed, too. I asked God to end this terrible, dark night soon. After a little while I knew that God wasn't going to answer either—so I went to sleep. I probably dreamed, but who knows what?

The morning was a blaze of light. I poked my head out of the blanket. The whole world was so bright my two eyes together took time to get used to it all. When I could see, I looked around hoping it was all different from the night past. Lucky it was. I spotted him down in the bowl digging like a coyote after a squirrel. I better walk over and see what we got this morning, I thought, and let's pretend there was no Bible and no songs and no tears around.

"So what did the old campers leave for us way back when?" I asked when I was close.

"Hay, hombre. These Indians were so smart. They made everything to last forever. Look at these points and these axes. Even now we could cut down a tree." He was *todo* happy. I hoped he wouldn't decide to do it. In just a little while I knew all the secrets about the ancients: how they made fire, how they scraped hides, who was buried with what, why they had moved away, and what they thought about us. I even felt it was my fault Antigua was now just bones.

It was close to noon when he was finally ready to go. He had a sack full of rocks and maybe even parts of Antigua's feet. We carried our things down the *mesita*, into the thick aspen forest and finally to the edge of the valley. We found a spring, cleaned out a little pool, and had a drink of water. From there on we stopped to rest only one time. He was in a hurry.

Tired and thirsty, we climbed the last little hill to the cabin. There Antigua was waiting with her no-choice smile.

"Hay, amiga, you are always so happy. You must know something we don't," he said to the skeleton as we walked up to the porch. I dropped my load and fell back on the plank floor. I must have fallen asleep.

"Oyes, hijo. It is almost time for you to start back," he said slowly. I sat up. It was already late afternoon.

"Just me? What about you?"

"I am not going. I need a few more days."

"But La Grande said for you to come home today."

"Ah! Tell her I will be down in three or four days, maybe Friday or Saturday." He gave me the look that said I should not argue with him.

I set out with about enough time to meet the truck at sunset, if I didn't stop to rest. As I walked along the trail, I tried to figure out what was wrong. Was he very mad at somebody? Maybe he was mad with La Grande for something. Or with my mother. Maybe he had gone crazy. "Crazy!" I said out loud, and it echoed back from the trees. "That's it. He's gone a little *loco!"* But how could El Grande get that way? How could I find out for sure? "Malvino!" I could go find him and ask him. He knew all about those things. Maybe he even did have powers. Maybe he could fix him, or at least tell me how. I was now running along the trail. I was excited. I was going to get an answer.

The sun was sinking behind the French Mesa by the time I crossed the last fence and headed to the rocky bank of the new road. La Grande and my mother were not there yet, but I was sure they would come. I sat on a stump near the road and watched the shadows of the trees get longer and longer and the Capulín Valley far below slowly turn gray. My plan was good.

TRECE

"Ay, qué hombre tan cabezudo." La Grande shook her head, sitting between me and the gear shift.

"I don't understand what is happening. Has he ever done this before? NO! Not since I've been his daughter," my mother answered her own question. "I guess he just doesn't care about his family anymore, or something," she said in Spanish since La Grande thought English was worse than disrespectful.

"No, he probably has too much work to do... and by himself, what can he do? Turn this truck around. I have to go help him," La Grande ordered.

"No, mama. You can't be out there in the mud and the rocks. And in the dark?" My mother didn't even let up on the gas. "You can't even see out of one eye anymore; *hay, Dios,* and the other one is already starting to go." She gave a quick brush to her forehead with her hand and then back tight on the wheel. The road was steep and curvy. "That is why we need him down. We have to decide when we are going to take you to the specialist," she added with a gentle touch to La Grande's lap.

My two mothers talked so much all the way down the mountain, I never got a chance to tell them everything. All I had said so far was that El Grande wasn't ready to come down; that even though I had told him it was important, he just said he would be down in a few days. What would they do if I told them all of it? They kept trying to figure out what was going on, but I guess they were so excited they didn't think of asking any more questions. Besides, El Grande wouldn't want me to say any more than I needed to. I remembered what he had said when the *gringos* got him drunk. Sometimes the less you say the better; or as he always said, *"Con pocas palabras, menos descalabras."*

When we got home my mother walked La Grande to her house and I went into our house. I was thirsty and tired and sleepy. I drank water and jumped into bed. In just a few minutes she was back, calling for me all over the house. I could hear her looking everywhere, as if she were looking for the cat to put it out for the night. In no time she exploded into the little room in the back of the house where I slept.

"No, no, no!" The no's came out of her mouth like a machine gun. She yanked the covers off my body. I was still in my dirty clothes. "Get up. You can't be sleepy, the chickens just barely went to sleep." I got up and sat on the edge of the bed, rubbing my eyes to pretend I was waking up. "All right, what is happening? I didn't want La Grande to hear everything; she can't be upset. It's bad for her eyes. But I know something is wrong. What was Papa doing?" You would have thought it was Naranjo the chota all over again. What could I do? I told just enough of the truth to keep it from being a sin. Deep into the night she asked questions. Something happens to your mind when you get no food, no clean clothes, no sleep, no peepee breaks, and lots of questions. I finally had to tell her about the skeleton. When I told her about it, she wrinkled her face and I didn't even tell her its name was Antigua. She made me tell the skeleton part twice. I don't know how many times she asked, "Are you sure?" When it was all over she said she was going up the mountain first thing in the morning. I said I was going, too, but she was quick to tell me I could not miss school. I begged. No way. School was the one thing she agreed on eye-to-eye with my father. What can you do when the rules won't bend? I went to bed hungry, tired, and praying for pleasant dreams.

Monday morning I was out the door before she was even ready to head up the mountain. At least it was the last week of school. Mrs. Majors had said it was time to clean things up and have everything ready for next year. I owed her a few corrected spelling words, but the last days of school would be easy. Right after school I would head over to Pedro's and look for Malvino to get my prayers answered. He could figure out what was going on with El Grande.

Mrs. Majors had fooled us. When the bell rang she sat us down and passed papers out. A test of everything we had studied all year, with no notice. Who could remember all that stuff? The capital of Montana? How many gallons is six quarts? Who discovered America? How much is one third and one half? What makes water go only downhill? Why do cats have whiskers? Who said, "Give me liberty or give me death?" Where did the first Americans land? and on and on. All morning long it took, but what could we do but try our best? Nobody wanted to be back in the same row of desks next year. It was almost noon when the test was finally over. We stumbled out into the sunshine, rubbing our eyes and our *nalgas,* too. We were all supposed to take our books with us and sit outside for the rest of the day erasing all the things we had written in them during the year. We'd written nasty things about the *gringo* kids and they had bad stuff about us. But today, Mrs. Majors even had extra erasers to make sure all the hate didn't cross the summer.

When the bell rang to end the day, I ran down the hill and headed toward Pedro's place along the edge of the deep arroyo. All the fears came to me. What if I couldn't find Malvino, or what if he did not know what to do? What if his powers were gone? I crossed the first fence and ran across an alfalfa field to a wood fence not far from Pedro's house. When I climbed the second fence, I spotted Malvino sitting on a ditch bank near the barn.

"Hey, Malvino! I am so happy to see you. What are you doing?" I asked, trying to be friendly. He didn't answer. I called to him again, this time louder.

"Shhhh. Don't disturb me. I am at peace with myself," he said, almost whispering. For a moment I stopped, but then I moved slowly up close to him.

"But I am not at peace, *hombre,*" I whispered. "I have a big problem I want to talk to you about." For a long while he just stared at the ground. "I know you have powers. I need them. I am sorry for saying that you didn't that time at the *molino*. I was wrong." Still nothing. He was making me pay, for sure.

Just as I was ready to give up, his head rose like a desert turtle and turned to look at me. His eyes were red as if he had been crying, or maybe he had not slept well.

"All right. I will talk to you, but only if you promise to believe everything I say. I do not want to waste my time with those who have no faith." He motioned for me to sit near him.

I told him the whole story: How El Grande had changed since the murder; all the time he had spent at the upper ranch; the deer he had killed with a bow and arrows; the skeleton; and that awful night at the *lagunitas* with the Bible. I told him he was still up there, not wanting to come down. Malvino never looked at me the whole time. He just kept pitching little pebbles, one at a time, into the flowing water of the small *acequia*. I didn't know what else to say, so I waited, and started pitching little rocks, too.

"He is an animal," Malvino said suddenly. "He is not people. He belongs to the mountain. Why do you want to change him to be like people?"

"He is not an animal! He is just acting strange." I got a little hot.

"*Bueno*. It is a mistake, to bring him from his world to yours. But if that is what you want, I will help you."

"Ok! How are you going to fix him?" I asked very excited and happy.

"Electricity."

"What? How?"

"Electricity," he repeated. "I have seen them come, one at a time into the chamber of wires. They go in kicking and screaming, they come out quiet and changed."

"Are you sure it will work?"

"*¡Fe, muchacho, fe!* You said you had faith in my power."

He was looking crazy-mean and the last thing I wanted was to get a loco man mad at me when I really needed him.

"I see things nobody else sees. I get messages from far away lands. And I send them, too." Malvino sounded so sure about all these things. With his hands he painted a picture of his powers in the air of the late afternoon as I sat on the warm ditch bank next to him and believed everything he said.

"How are we going to save El Grande?" I asked respectfully, trying not to set him off again.

"I will send a message to my institution and tell them to get the chamber of wires ready. You have to get him there."

"I have to get him there? How?"

"You will figure out a way! *¡FE, hombre, FE!*"

He was getting mad at me so I figured I wouldn't ask for anything more. I thanked Malvino for his help and told him that someday I would pay him back for all his help.

He just looked up at me and shook his head. "And bring me gum, too," he said, adding to my bill.

I headed back the same way I had come. I wasn't really happy with all that he had said to me, but when you don't have regular answers, faith is good enough. I walked across the alfalfa field trying to figure out how I was ever going to get El Grande to the chamber of wires.

When I got to the deep arroyo, I took the trail that led to the opposite bank and headed to the store. As I came around the corner of the house, I saw the old truck parked in front of the store, splattered with mud and even a few weeds stuck on the tires. Mother had got to the top of the mountain, got stuck, and had to turn around and come home, I thought. I ran onto the porch and into the store.

"Hey, *amigo!*" El Grande yelled from near the potbelly where he was sitting cutting an apple with his knife. I looked at him and then at my mother. For a moment I didn't know what to say.

"What are you doing here?" I asked as I walked toward him.

"Eating apples!" He laughed like he had said something funny.

"We just got back. That road is awful... it's not even a road, it's a cow trail. But thank the good Lord we got out," my mother said as she glanced quickly at the sky. El Grande looked fine. But after a little while his eyes met mine and he nodded toward the door. He stood up, stretched his back, and told my mother he was going across the road. I followed him out. We met in the shed.

"Have you seen La Grande yet?" I asked.

"No. I'm going in now. How much do they know?" he asked.

"Not too much. I had to tell my mother about the skeleton. I thought I might go to hell if I didn't tell that much."

"Bueno. 'Stá bien." He looked at me to make sure I was telling the truth. "Go home. Tomorrow, after school, we will talk some more. You are a man. A good man," he said.

I ran across the road, back to the store. Three *gringos* from the *molino* were buying food and cigarettes. I could tell my mother was happy that they were there doing business.

On the fourth day before school was out, Mrs. Majors yawned and scratched her belly. Those who owed her work rubbed their eyes and hoped for the world to end soon. The rest of us worked on our books with smoking-hot erasers.

By late morning somebody pushed somebody. Then somebody spit. One jumped in to help another. Then two more jumped in. When two of us shoved one of them through one of the holes of the two-holer in the back of the school, it was all-out war. The only one who had trouble picking sides was Tusa, the honorary *vaquero.* He picked himself up after some-body had laid him out with a stray kick to the back of his knees and ran to report the first riot the Capulín Valley had ever had to Mrs. Majors.

> "*¡Mátalo, mátalo!*"
> "Kick the sheat out o'him!"
> "*¡Dale una patada en los huevos!*"
> "You damn greasers!"
> "*¡Ayúdame con este gordito!*"

Dust, weeds, rocks, shoes and even blood flew through the air in the schoolyard and unless you were a girl, you were in a fight for your life. The *gringo* kids were fewer but they were tough. The battle lasted until Mrs. Majors stormed out of the schoolhouse, still carrying a bucket of soapy water in one hand and a dirty rag in the other. Nobody heard her first demand to stop the war, but when the spray of soapy water, followed by the bucket, landed on us, a pile of dusty kids, we all knew the fight was over. A few more groans and shoves, but most of us just stood up and checked ourselves for lumps and leaks.

"What the ail's goin' on here?" she howled with her thun-der voice. "Who's fightin' who? Who started all this?" Every-body pointed to everybody else. Her face was red and her hands were shaking. "All right, if nobody's goin 'ta 'fess... I want all of you to line up against the wall, facing it. Then I want you to kneel down like you're prayin' and put your head between the wall and the ground. Hurry up!"

Like prisoners, we did what we were told. We all got on our knees and put our foreheads right up against the wall of the school where the tender weeds had already sprouted. It happens that in this position your butt is sticking way out in the air. She had set up a long row of them.

Mrs. Majors invited all the girls to come outside to watch the show. Then she went into the schoolhouse and brought out her paddle, the one that had "THE LAW" written on it. Up and down the line she marched, giving each one of us our turn with the paddle. Each time the girls clapped. Every few swats she asked if anybody had anything to say. Nobody spoke. Then she got the girls to chant: " Hit 'em again, harder, harder! Hit 'em again, harder, harder!" My butt began to feel like it had hot marbles rolling over it, but I couldn't give up. Nobody did.

At long last she either got tired or worried. She told us to stand up and face her, keeping an orderly line against the wall. She smiled at us with an evil slant to her mouth as the beads of sweat ran down her face and her huge bosom heaved up and down. Her flower-printed dress was wet under the armpits. She turned and looked at the girls; they giggled. For a long while she marched back and forth along the line, looking at each one of us like a horse trader searching for signs of worms. Finally, she spoke.

"I've seen this thing a'comin' for quite a while now. I am ashamed of you boys. I thought you knew better than to fight like this. Look at you: dusty, dirty, bloody, ugly. I guess I haven't taught you anything about life. I guess you don't understand there are all kinds of people in the world—light ones, dark ones, even black ones. All created equal by God. Two eyes, nose, a heart, and a mind, and all supposed to speak English. 'With justice for all,' the pledge of allegiance sez. Some of you have always lived here and some of us have come from far away, but that don't matter. Someday all of us will be gone. Dead, and that's what makes us all the same, too. You boys are asking for that day to come sooner than it should. I don't know what else I can say to you, so I want each of you to go over and shake hands with whoever you hit or wanted to hit in this fight... C'mon."

Each one of us went over and shook limp hands with the *gringo* kids. Some had swollen eyes or cut lips. Everybody was dusty.

"All right, now listen to me," she started again. "I hope all of you look at each other. This fightin' is an awful thing. I have tried my best. What else can I do?" She looked at each one of us, then turned and looked at the girls. Tears began rolling down her face. Some of the girls started crying, too. She wiped her face with her hand. "I want all of you kids to go into the schoolhouse, get everything that belongs to you and go home. I don't want to see you anymore. School is over."

The end had never come like this. The last day of school had always been a happy celebration. Suddenly I felt sad and I wanted the three days more of school. I felt sorry for Mrs. Majors.

On my way out the door I saw the Tusa heading toward the trail that led to the *molino.*

"Hey, have a good summer, *vaquero,"* I yelled. He turned and gave me a little half-wave with his hand full of books.

"See you next year," he said. He didn't seem to be mad.

I headed down the trail toward the deep arroyo. I had walked this way with trouble on my mind before and I hoped that Rosa Velásquez would appear in the form of a coyote again. Maybe she would do something to make me feel better. But when I got to the arroyo there was no coyote and I still felt bad when I got home. Through the window I saw that El Grande was helping my mother move some boxes of cans from one part of the store to another.

"What are you doing home so early? What happened to your clothes?" my mother asked as I walked in.

"We had a big fight. All of us against all the *gringo* kids. Mrs. Majors ended school early and here I am," I went with the whole truth right away. If the leather *reata* is next, let it come, I thought. They looked at each other.

"Oh, my Lord," my mother sighed. *"¿Qué vamos a hacer con este chamaco?"* she added as she turned to El Grande. He looked me over for a moment, like maybe I had the hoof and mouth, and then called me outside. He signaled for me to follow him. As we walked across the road toward the smokehouse, I had the very strong feeling it was going to be one more visit with the leather *reata.* But when we were inside, something I wasn't ready for happened. He told me to sit down.

"You are the only witness to my struggle. My fight. And I am the one that sees yours. We are at the moment of truth. You and me. I am between the old ways and the new. I am the bear and the deer and the eagle. Free.

"You are young and full of hope. You have the spirit of the mountain, but the wind of the new. The burden of the future is yours to carry. The great adventure is now upon your shoulders." He looked at me with watery eyes and a shake in his hand. I didn't know what to do. He almost scared me. "Here. This is yours." He handed me the leather *reata,* coiled around his arm like a treasured snake. "It has done its duty." I reached and took it in my hand and folded it, back and forth, like S's next to my arm. I could feel the power, the grace of the fine leather, black with sweat. "What I want in return is a promise. I want my dignity... my respect. You must help me to die with honor."

I looked into his face and I saw the pain. So, too, the strength of his words. Time stopped. I closed my eyes. I saw him again. He does not need the chamber of wires. He really *is* the bear and the deer and the eagle, I thought.

"I will do it. Until the Lord comes to claim my soul, I will do everything you say. I will help you." As I said the words I felt the sadness and the weight of my promise. Could I really do as I had said?

CATORCE

"Education is the only thing that counts in life," my father always said, especially when I was just staring at my homework.

"Working the land with your bare hands and not depending on any other man for anything is the only way for a man to live," El Grande always said, especially when I was being lazy.

"I want all of you kids to go into the schoolhouse, get everything that belongs to you and go home. School is over," Mrs. Majors had said three days too early, and for the first time I had felt sad that school was over.

All these thoughts had been bothering me during the night, in my dreams or while I just lay there in the dark, awake. The world always looks worse in the dark, I tried to tell myself. It didn't help. So, on the morning of the third to last day of school, with no school to go to, I got up earlier than usual and went across the road to see how El Grande was doing. I prayed that he was better than the day before when he had even put me in charge of my own *disciplina!*

I met La Grande at the door and she didn't even wait for me to ask. She said he had left very early. All the work he had to do at the upper rancho was bothering him.

"But why didn't he take me with him? School is out," I pleaded with a wrinkled face. La Grande just threw her hands up as if she had run out of words. Then she ordered me to go in and have breakfast. As I sat at the table eating my hot tortillas, eggs, and beans, I tried to make sense out of my confusing life. School was over before its time, El Grande had left me behind, giving me the *reata* as if I didn't need it anymore; and worst of all, the baseball game we always had on the last day of school wasn't going to happen. Who would organize it? Mrs. Majors didn't want to see us ever again. Not even La Grande's food tasted good that morning. Wait a minute, I thought. We'll do it ourselves!

I ran out the door, onto the road, and headed for the bridge. That was the place the guys always hung around, *abuelo* time, murder time, any time. Sure enough, Ricardo and Leo were there, sitting on the edge with their feet hanging over the side, throwing little rocks into the water below.

"Hey, let's have us a baseball game."

"Hey, yeah. Why not?"

"Against who?"

"How about the *gringo* kids?"

"Naw. They're mad."

"Well, let's go see anyway."

Before the last rock hit the water we were on our way to the *molino* looking for a game. In half an hour or less we were at the edge of the *molino* community, not far from the heat of the scrap burner, looking for a friendly face. Up the road came a stick-like person toward us, female. Who else? Brains herself, Susie Kimball.

"Hey, where's Tusa and them other guys?" one of us yelled when she was close enough. She stopped and looked. Questions in her mind, we could tell.

"Are you guys here to pick another fight, or what?" she asked with a little anger in her voice.

"No. No, of course not," Leo said in very fine English. "We are merely here to speak of baseball," he added. We all laughed, which didn't help. Susie looked some more, with a wrinkled forehead.

"You wait here. I'll go get them," she said as she broke into a full gallop back up the dusty road. We felt pretty good, getting brains to do us a little favor. We looked at each other, spit on the ground, and waited. But not for long. Up the road we saw dozens of guys in a dust cloud, some our size and other giants we had never seen before. They were closing on us fast.

"A la madre, let's run for it!" somebody howled. Just then we saw five, maybe six men running from the lumber stacks toward us, too.

"No more fights! All you boys quit that sheat." The men ran between us and the dozens of *gringo* kids and giants just in time to stop something before it started. For a moment everybody waited to see what was going to happen next.

"We're here just to see about a friendly game of baseball," Leo said in his good English.

"We'll play ya, ya little squirts," one big, freckle-faced kid slobbered. "You just name the place and the time and we'll be there to kick your little naglas." I think he meant *nalgas.*

"All right, how about Saturday, one o'clock?" I said, without even thinking. Why then? I don't know. It just came out.

"Saturday it is. We'll play right over there," another said, pointing to a brand-new baseball field with backstop and everything. The *gringos* had no doubt used their big yellow machines to level off the chamisal into a fine ball diamond. It was like nothing we had even seen before.

That night there was a meeting at the store. Grown men, the guys, my mother, me, and even a few old people, women, too. It was like the bell for school had rung and the whole village was ready for the first lesson.

"We have just two days to practice," Bernabé told the group. It wasn't as if we didn't know anything about baseball. The village marrieds had always played the village singles on the weekends, from the time the snow melted in the spring to fall. Sunday afternoons the whole village turned out to watch. It was the only proper time to yell insults. The wives cheered for their husbands, and the single ladies cheered for the singles' team. Some no doubt hoped their cheering would get them to the other side!

Around the potbelly, the plans quickly took shape. Who has bats? Who has extra mitts? What are we going to use for uniform? White t-shirts somebody said.

The next day, some of the men sneaked out of work at the *molino* early to start baseball practice. The game had become so important me, and the guys weren't even sure if we would get to play. Sometimes a good idea can breathe on its own. Practice lasted until the last bit of sun had disappeared behind the French Mesa. By Saturday morning, it was clear who was going to start, and only José Torres had made the starting lineup. The rest of us "squirts" would just have to hope for a break.

Close to noon on Saturday, the store was full of people buying Coke, candy, crackers, cheese, picnic stuff. Some brought their *lonche* from home and it smelled good, like fresh tortillas. Not since the murder of Luke Evans had there been so many excited people in the place. My mother was making money like crazy. But soon men, women, little babies, dogs, even a cat or two, piled onto pickup trucks for the ride to the *molino* ball field.

A huge dust cloud covered the lower valley, kicked up by every available truck and car carrying people to the big, big game. As they arrived, each parked in a neat row along the first-base line. The *gringos* and their fancy trucks, some with duals, lined the third-base side. Even before any players took the field, a few barbs were tossed from one side to the other. When the *gringos* took the field for warmup, a huge cheer, car horns, a shotgun blast or two showed their spirit. They had blue uniforms, numbers and everything. On our side people were spreading blankets, picking spots to get the best view. Dogs were barking here and there. The *gringos* seemed to warm up forever, When our team finally took the field, dressed in Levi's and white t-shirts, the noise was deaf-making.

> *"Orale, cho dem."*
> "Les go, les go, les go."
> *"Que se watchen esos panzones."*
> "C'mon, Tony, you too, José."

Almost an hour late, the umpire, a *gringo*, yelled, "Batters up." Both sides went crazy. People yelled, horns blew, dogs barked. The *gringos* were up. The first pitch was a ball and everybody's nerves loosened just a little. Second pitch, a blast over the center fielder for a triple. Just lucky, just lucky, were the noises from our side. The *gringos* were clapping smugly. The second batter hit a one-hopper to right field and the run scored. Next, a popup to second. Then another blast to center. Finally, at the end of the first half of the first, it was five to zero. Up and down, one, two, three. We didn't even touch the ball with the bat. It was starting to look like a very long afternoon. Some even glanced behind them to see if anyone was parked in their way. In the bottom of the fourth, one of our guys hit a long fly into center field, but it was caught. Hope that we could at least hit the ball spread a little. But the *gringos* were rolling. It was eight to nothing.

"Hey, beaners, missin' yore *siesta?*"

"How come ye'all playing in your pajamas?"

"Why don't you use one of them tortillas for a mitt?"

"Go home, practice. Come back next week! Ha, ha, ha."

Finally, in the bottom of the sixth, three singles in a row. Nine to one. Bottom of the seventh, still 9-1. A single and two walks, their pitcher was getting tired. Then our very own José

Torres, the sixth grader with a beard, hit a blast to left with the bases loaded and ran the bases like he was headed for lunch. Suddenly it was 9-5. Our side went crazy.

"Ok, now stick it, blondie," somebody yelled to the lady across third base who had been giving us the worst time.

"Abranse, piojos, aquí viene el peine," somebody else yelled.

"Hey, *panza de sandía,* you gonna shattup now?" Malvino, of all people, yelled to some crazy guy across the field. Everybody laughed.

Roberto stepped to the plate. The cheers got even louder. First pitch, a long, high fly to center. The center fielder just parked under it and waited. The ball landed exactly in the pocket of his mitt—and bounced out: 9-6. In the eighth the *gringos* had the bases loaded with two outs, but a sizzler to short was caught for the third out. People felt the relief of a visit to the you know what. We were up and down, they were up and down, which got us to the bottom of the ninth, the score still 9-6.

Some people don't believe in miracles, but that day, in the middle of the *chamisal,* next to the *molino,* not far from the village of Capulín, two of them happened back to back. With the bases loaded, two outs, two strikes and no balls, Bernabé stepped into a bad pitch and hit a little blooper over the first baseman. The fielder ran for the ball, but out of nowhere Hitler beat him by half a step. The German Shepherd took the ball in his mouth like a fancy dog with training, and hid under his master's truck. Four runs scored, the *gringos* ranted, we cheered for Hitler.

The umpire held his hands high over his head signaling to stop the game. Was it 9-10? No! He pointed to Bernabé and sent him back to third. "Obstruction, the score is nine-nine," he said. We went crazy. The *gringos* started going crazy, too. Our players ran to the middle of the field and surrounded the umpire, no doubt ready to kill him. Then the *gringos* surrounded our players. Another huge fight, we all thought. But then came the second miracle.

Perhaps nobody had noticed it, or it just appeared. Overhead, a black cloud suddenly let loose with a flash of lightning, followed by a loud thunderbolt, like Mrs. Majors' voice in the early morning. All the people looked up, but then back to the fight that was about to happen. A miracle. Huge hailstones began pelting the field, some the size of eggs. Then more thunder. Everybody ran for cover. Nobody could believe it. People hid in cars, under trucks, in trucks, no matter who they belonged to. Hitler was still under one, too.

By the time it was over the field was inches deep in hail ice. People came out from vehicles with fogged up windows to see what had happened. Nobody cheered, or even talked. It was like everybody was waking up from a bad dream. In a little while the umpire went to the middle of the field, kicked a few footloads of hail. "I declare this game a rainout, or hail-out, I guess. It ends in a tie at nine-nine. We will need another game to decide this contest." Both sides booed, but I think we along the first base line were more or less happy.

The rest of the afternoon was a muddy mess full of questions. How could such things have happened? What possessed that dog? somebody asked. And what about the hail, so sudden? The weather is changing a lot around here since all the smoke, somebody smart said. It was God, an old woman offered.

It was only the first game with the *gringos*. The men working at the *molino* worked it out: Every week, on Sunday, a game with the *gringos*. At the end of the summer whoever had won the most games would buy the beer and soda for the united community picnic. The games were to become the most important thing to talk about all summer. Everyone of us worked on his game, hoping to get to play someday. The men started ordering mitts, balls, bats, and even shoes from the Sears book.

QUINCE

It was dawn when I heard the first noises and smelled the first perfume. The house was full of chatter, drawers opening and closing, light everywhere, giggles here and there, and complaints from me.

"Can't you tell I'm trying to sleep, or what?" Nobody listened to me. My little sister Lydia was running around squeaking. I could hear my mother talking to La Grande about something that wouldn't fit because she had gotten too fat. La Grande proposed to just let it out a little *aquí y allá.* One of them said that it was going to be hotter in Duke City than in Capulín, so not too heavy on the sweaters.

"At no time do I want you to leave me alone with those doctors," I heard La Grande say.

"Don't worry, *mamacita,* I'll be with you day and night," my mother assured her, while I was hoping they would leave me alone at least in the night when I was trying to sleep.

"It's getting late. Before you know it Miguel will be here, so you better hurry with the packing," I heard my father announce from another room. With all of that noise I figured I might as well get up and catch a little of the action myself. I walked into the room where they were busy getting ready for the big trip to the *specialista* for La Grande's eyes. Never had I seen so many shoes, curlers, brushes, and make-up in one place. You would have thought somebody was getting married.

Miguel Guerra had been hired by my father to take the two women to Duke City in his new sedan car. Miguel had had his leg blown off in the war. The Veterans had made him a new one out of wood, and every month he got a check in the mail. No wonder he could have a new car without even working.

My father had been in a kind of war, too, being a teacher just like Mrs. Majors for some forty years. I had heard talk around the kitchen about retirement, but I didn't really know what it was or what it might do to me. But when he said he could not go to Duke City because he had to stay behind and get the store ready to close, it hit me that something serious was happening. Even more important, he said he also had to help El Grande sell the timber in the rancho to the *molino.* How come nobody told me what was going on? I wondered.

But now, it was suitcase-loading time. Miguel had pulled up to the gas pump and I was told to fill'er up. The trunk was stuffed with women's things, and in a few minutes my mother, La Grande, *la consentida, and* my little sister Lydia were all kissing me, redstick all over my face. My mother gave a little one to my father on the cheek, which hardly ever happened, and got into the car, La Grande in the middle. Lydia was loaded into the back seat. They drove off and I felt a little sad. I wouldn't see them again for weeks.

"It feels funny being alone with you, everybody else gone," I told my father after we had had a little breakfast and a getting-acquainted talk.

"Yes, it is," he said as he read from an old newspaper. " I think you should have a choice: Stay here and work with me in the store, or go to La Mesa and spend some time with El Grande," he said after a while.

"Oh! I thought I was supposed to go help El Grande? Yes, I want to go." He looked a little hurt, but who would want to miss the hunting and riding around the mountains looking for strays? There was hard work to do, too, but I was used to it. And besides, strange as he was being, El Grande needed me more, I thought.

In the middle of the afternoon, my father dropped me off at the top of the mountain, the same spot where I had waited for my mother and La Grande to pick me up many weeks before. I picked up the wagon trail and headed into the thick oaks and aspen. I got into the dark shadows of all that *mamacita* nature was pushing out of the forest floor and the memories came. It was like the day I had run into Antigua hanging from the porch. What am I going to find today? I wondered. Sometimes your mind feels like you've done the same thing before.

When I came around the bend of the road where I could see the potato patch, I saw them all. The pigs. Tall among her snotty friends, La Aprovechada, digging for leftovers from last year. Now what? I worked my way along the edge of the woods so she wouldn't see me, until I came to the end—no more woods between me and the cabin. I took a deep breath and blasted off across the clearing for the cabin. The gray pig and I streaked across a bare spot of the rocky mountains. I got to the porch in plenty of time. Yellow teeth flashing, she arrived too late to do anything but grunt and admit defeat. La Aprovechada was a good sport. She flashed her blonde eyelashes at me and Antigua, still hanging there, and headed back to the potato patch.

"*¡¿Qué pasa, hombre?!*" El Grande hollered as he stepped outside onto the porch, laughing. He had seen the whole thing.

"Why didn't you come out and help me? I could be pig-chewed right now," I said, a little mad. He laughed some more and shook my hand.

"You are a man, a fast one, too, and you can take care of yourself," he said as he gave me a slap on the back. We went into the cabin and sat down at the table for a glass of water. We had a way of drinking together when it counted. He wanted to know how La Grande was doing. I told him everything, especially about La Grande's trip and about the baseball game with the *gringos*. We talked until even the coyotes had given up for the night.

We spent the next few days walking the ranch with a *gringo* from the Duke City Lumber Corporation, the owner of the *molino*. Every morning, about sunrise, he showed up at the cabin with his tools: a marking ax and a can of orange paint. We walked with him all over the rancho, marking the trees to be cut. The *gringo* was very smart. He explained how to tell which trees were the best, which ones had disease and even how old they were. He explained about watershed, erosion, canopy and boardfeet—words I had never heard before. Even worse, it was hard to translate to El Grande, but he didn't seem to be real interested anyway. Every time we came to a tree to be cut, the man shaved a flat spot on the bark and hit it with the back of his ax, which left a mark saying, USFS. Then he painted an orange line around the tree. When the *gringo* hit the tree, El Grande wrinkled his face and got stiff, like the man was hitting him. I was proud that the *gringo* found so many of our pine trees good enough to cut.

"When they are finished, my land is going to look like a desert," El Grande said one night as we sat on the porch looking at the stars.

"But think of all the money the *molino* is going to give you," I said. "You will be able to buy whatever you want, even a truck." He didn't answer me. He just gave me a grunt, like one of the hogs, and went inside.

It wasn't long before the big yellow machines came. First the bulldozers. Great big things. They cut roads to every part of the rancho where before you could only go on a horse or walk. The sounds of the big machines echoed from the cliffs and the smell of diesel was everywhere. Our old trails disappeared in places. Frõm the new roads everything looked different. What had been far away was now close, what was close we could not find. The roads had changed everything. Behind the bulldozers came the log cutters with their chain saws. Huge trees, some the *gringo* said were two hundred years old, crashed to the ground in a few minutes. Branches were cut off and stacked, then the tree I had known as a friend was cut to length and turned into a log. Finally, the loaders and the trucks came. Every truck carried a dozen or more logs to be turned into boards at the *molino.*

It was a miracle, the work they did. Every day I got up and ran to were the action was. I watched the forest change before my eyes. I forgot about horses and strays and pigs and all other rancho work. El Grande? He didn't seem to mind that I was gone all day and wasn't helping him. I couldn't understand why he wouldn't come to watch with me.

One morning, as I trotted along the dusty road, a logging truck came up behind me.

"Hey, kid! Where you goin'?" the driver yelled out the window as he slowed.

"Up there. "I pointed toward the chain-saw noise."

"You wanna ride?"

"Yeah. Sure I do."

"Hop on, kid, fast!" I ran, climbed two steps, and reached high for the door handle and got in.

"Name's George," he said as he stuck his hand out. I told him my name and we shook. George looked exactly like a pirate I had seen in a book once: Skinny, long hook nose, most of his teeth gone, his eyes sunk deep in his head and a red rag tied around his balding head. "Want a chew off of my plug here?" he asked as he offered his Days Work tobacco. I said no; he laughed. The noise of the engine was so loud I could hardly hear the pirate, and so bumpy I could just barely stay on the torn seat. We drove along the road yelling a word or two at a time. Around a bend we came close to a huge yellow loader waiting just off the road. George slowed down. "You can ride with me as long as you want, but if I say DUCK, you dive to the floorboard, ok? And if I say RUN, you get out and run like hell and get lost, you hear?" I said ok and slid to the floor to show him how fast I could do it. He thought I was funny.

We made three trips to the *molino* that day, loaded with logs. George's truck was big and strong and noisy and stinky and wonderful. In one day I learned about double-clutching, downshifting, and dual-range. At noon George pulled off the road and parked the truck under a tree. He reached behind the seat and pulled out a sack with a can of Spam and a loaf of bread.

"Now we gonna have us a trucker sandwich," he said as he opened the can with a key. "You open the bread, boy." I pulled out four slices and he cut us some chunks of meat. By the time we started eating, the bread had turned dusty brown from our dirty hands. Who cares? Truckers are tough, I thought. He got a water bag that was hanging on the side mirror. He took a big gulp until water and dust ran down both sides of his face. "Drink?" he offered. I did the same.

On our last ride up the mountain, George said he liked me as his sidekick. He offered me his plug of Day's Work again. This time I decided to try a little. Since he had been teaching me how to spit, I figured I might as well do it for real. I took a big plug and chewed it like candy. At first it tasted sweet, so I swallowed the juice. The sweet changed to the taste of weeds, and then to straight awful. By the time we reached the top of the mountain, I was sick as a dying person. I leaned out the window and gave up the trucker sandwich. George laughed and pounded on the steering wheel. I sat on the torn seat hoping to either die or just get off the bumpy truck. Finally, at the junction with the wagon road, he brought the truck to a screeching halt.

"Wail, this is the end of the trail for you, *amigo,*"he yelled with a laugh. "One last lesson before you die: chew, spit, but don't swallow." He pointed his crooked finger at me and let out one more laugh.

I had just enough time to roll off the truck to the dusty road before the Day's Work struck again. I didn't even answer, except for a weak wave of my hand. He waved back through the big, rearview mirror as the diesel jerked up the new road.

By the end of the week, we had hauled a thousand years of logs and I had learned to chew without getting sick. I had even learned the gears and how to work the big hand brake. Soon, I'm going to be driving this truck, I thought.

After supper, El Grande and I sat at the table talking about all that was happening. I told him about my rides with George and all about our truck. For a long time he just leaned back on his chair and listened to my excited stories.

"We have work to do here on the ranch. You are going to have to help me," he said. "Just for a few days. Then I am going to take you on a ride. A very important ride."

"I will help you, Grande. Just tell me what to do," I said, almost happy we were going to do some rancho work. "What kind of ride are we going to take?"

"The time has come when you must learn the trail down into the *cañón.* To the Río Chama and on to the Cerro del Pedernal," he said seriously. He said it was a sacred place, where all men, no matter what language or color, could go in peace. The only place in the whole world. For hundreds of years, Indians from all tribes met at the foot of the *cerro* to trade and to make peace. There, they gathered the black flint to make arrow points and the *palo* duro to make bows. He said I was now old enough to learn the secrets of the Cerro del Pedernal. "It will take four days, going and coming," he said. I had heard stories of the *cerro* and I was excited to go.

We spent the next few days fixing the old loading chute in the *potrero.* At the end of the summer the cattle buyers would come. Every year they came and all the calves were sold. This year it was going to be different. El Grande said that the whole herd was going to be sold. Calves, cows, bulls, old, ugly, everything. I couldn't believe it. I asked him what we would do about milk and cheese and meat. He just said we would buy it at a store. We worked hard, fixing the chute, mending fences and digging trenches. Toward the end of the week, he let me ride down with George for a reward, hauling logs to the *molino.*

The bumpy, stinky ride was great. At the *molino* I saw some of the *gringo* kids. They were watching us unload our logs. I sat in the truck while George loosened the chains.

"Hey, what are you doing?" one of the kids yelled.

"I'm hauling logs, what do you think?" I said smugly.

They came over to the truck to see if I was real, no doubt. We talked while George fixed something under the truck. They asked me if I was going to the big game. It was halfway through the season and the teams were even. "I will if I can get off work," I said.

In the late afternoon of the day before our ride to the *cerro,* I came home to the cabin with trouble on my mind. I wanted to ride with El Grande to the *cerro,* but what about the game? I would miss the game. But then, I would hurt his feelings. What would I do? I figured I would just ask him what to do.

"I have tried to teach you to decide things yourself. I cannot tell you which way to choose. You are old enough. You must decide," he said calmly.

I hoped I wasn't so old.

We cooked. We ate. We cleaned. We sat at the table, yawning. We were about to go to sleep when suddenly it was clear. That game was going to happen only once. The *cerro* would be there forever.

"Okay. I figured it out. I want to ride down with my friend George and stay for the game. I will come back Monday. Okay? We can go to the *cerro* another time. Ok?" I was *todo* nervous.

"Are you sure about your decision?" he asked.

"Yes. Yes, sir, I am..." I started to explain, but he stopped me.

"I do not want to hear your reasons. Your decision is yours. You must stand for what you decide and what you believe. In the end you always stand alone. You are born alone and you die alone. You alone are the master of your dignity, your honor, the way you live, and the way you die. As for me, I will die with dignity." All of this he said in a loud voice, like he was at the church, in front of all the citizens of Capulín.

When he finished he walked into the other room and went to sleep. He didn't look at me or say anything more. In a little while I went in behind him and lay down on the little cot across the room from him. He was snoring. I could not sleep. I wondered if he was going to get strange again.

The next morning when I woke up he was gone. Had he ridden to the *cerro* alone? I felt bad for not going with him. For me, it was the right decision, but it was the worst decision I had ever had to make.

For the entire summer, El Grande never came off his mountain. I took notes to him from my father, like when Duke City wanted him to sign for a check. When the cattle buyers were going to come. A letter from La Grande. He just said for my father to take care of it all. No need for him to bother. Just send word what to do next.

The big yellow machines pushed way beyond the rancho, past the *lagunitas* and almost to the end of the mesa. The logging trucks were taking a different road now, so no more riding with George. In the last part of summer I spent the days with El Grande, looking for strays, counting cows, and getting ready for the day when the buyers would come. El Grande was in a fun mood. He made jokes about how La Aprovechada would be turned into bacon for the city folks and they wouldn't know what they were really eating; how he was going to buy a fancy car to drive on all the roads and get to know the forest again; how he was going to hunt bears by shooting them from his car as they crossed the road.

Early on the day before the buyers came, El Grande saddled up and rode away with Antigua strapped to his saddle. I watched from the window. I knew he would be mad if he found out, but as soon as he was into the forest, I ran down the trail, crossed the fence and followed him on foot. His horse was easy to track and I could soon see where he was headed. The *lagunitas.* I was sweating and puffing, but we got there almost at the same time. I found a spot behind some bushes where I could watch. With a little shovel he had brought, he made the hole from where Antigua had come deeper. He shaped it nicely, then he put her in. It looked like he wanted her turned a certain way, I guess on her side. He put leaves and twigs on top of her. Finally he went to his horse and got the hex-barrel .30—.30 rifle and laid it in the hole with the skeleton.

I almost threw up as I watched him bury the Indian woman with his gun. What was he doing? I was all confused. When he was finished, he looked up, across the *cañon* of the Río Chama and beyond to La Mesa De Las Viejas, as if he were smelling the wind. In a little while, he got on his horse and rode back toward the cabin.

The next morning three huge trucks rolled right up to the place where the cattle would be loaded. Behind them were my father and Tusa, and four or five other trucks with people from Capulín. It seemed nobody wanted to miss the action. Tusa grabbed the last saddled horse tied to the fence and rode out to where me and El Grande were working the herd. I felt proud of him for still being the *vaquero* we had made out of him.

One by one the cattle were checked for brands and tags as they walked up the chute and onto the truck. When one trailer was full, the next truck was backed up to the chute. Dust, mooing, whistling, and busy talk filled the morning air. The smell of horse sweat and cow shit, too.

By the middle of the morning, the checking, counting and loading were done. Three big trailers, loaded with all of El

Grande's cattle, were ready to roll somewhere far away. The *gringo* buyers, my father, and El Grande stood together looking at papers with the count. When everything was agreed upon, one of the *gringos* pulled a pen from his pocket and started writing a check. Suddenly everybody got quiet. Who would want to miss the moment when all those cows got turned into a piece of paper. When the check was done, who knows for how much, the *gringo* handed it to El Grande, but he was quick to hand it to my father without even looking at it.

"Don Ezequiel, it's been a real pleasure doin' bidness with you, sir," one *gringo* said as he shook hands with El Grande.

"*Bueno, amigo.* Make sure you take good care of my cows, because they don't speak any English," El Grande said with a little smile. Everybody who understood Spanish laughed. My father translated and the *gringos* laughed, too. One of them put his hand on El Grande's shoulder.

"Don't you worry, *amigo.* Where they are goin' all they need to know is how to smile." Almost everybody laughed again.

It was over. The big diesel trucks rolled away from the chute and out of the *potrero,* leaving a cloud of gray dust. The men watched until the last one disappeared behind the trees, then they all paid their respects to El Grande and drove away. Tusa rode with George back to the *molino.* Finally, El Grande, my father and I were left alone.

Without saying anything, El Grande unsaddled all the horses and threw the saddles into the back of my father's old Ford truck. He took Jerky, the old bay mare, put her inside the fence and turned her loose to graze. Then, one by one, he turned all the other horses loose, outside the fence. Finally, the only one left tied up was Smokey, the *pinto.* Smokey was a wild horse, and even though he had been saddle broke for years, whenever he got a chance he would still run away. For him, El Grande had special respect, maybe because he had never been able to fully break him. Finally, El Grande walked up to Smokey and took the bridle off. He grabbed him by his messy mane and rubbed his sweaty shoulder with his hand.

"Now you are free, *caballo pinto.* Go to where your spirit calls you. The *chamisales* from where I took you long ago, they are yours again. But remember one thing, *bronco,* if one day I am at the gates of heaven and I need a good horse to get in, I will know where to find you. *Adiós, mi pinto.*" The horse walked away slowly, as if he were not sure, his nose smelling the ground. But in a few yards, he broke into a trot and then a gallop. All the other horses followed.

The last roundup was over. The three of us climbed into my father's truck and headed down the bumpy road toward Capulín.

DIECISEIS

There was no talk in the truck all the way down. Not even a little something about how tired we were. But I knew El Grande's insides weren't feeling so good because he looked like he wanted to whistle.

Finally, we arrived back at the store. My father turned the truck and backed it up to El Grande's saddle shed. First we unloaded saddles, then we all went into El Grande's house to make sure no thieves had been over for a little visit. No thieves, but it was cold even if it was summer. Dusty, too, as if nobody had cleaned in weeks, and the kitchen smelled as though it hadn't been cooked in for a long time. On all the window sills the geraniums, the ones that La Grande always picked at to keep them pretty, she said, were dead. Brown sticks reached out of the pots with their wrinkled leaves like hands asking for a little water. Not even the holy kind could bring them back. El Grande walked around the house and then declared it in *buena condición* and we left, to cross the road. As we walked I knew that his insides were hurting because everything was so alone, so *abandonado*.

Our house was just as dusty and the store was packed up. Boxes everywhere. There were still a few stacks of things left from the bargain days, no doubt soon to become bargains of bargains. The big freezer that had welcomed real ice cream to Capulín was still there, but it was not even plugged in. When I opened it just for a quick peek, it looked like a giant coffin with the smell of old cheese. I went to the money drawer behind the counter just in case, but it was empty. Only the potbelly was standing strong in the middle of the store; it hadn't moved anywhere and I could still see the stains of somebody's tobacco spit when it had been hot.

I found the two men sitting at the table in the kitchen, looking at a bunch of mail. Just like the teacher that he was, my father read a letter from my mother out loud. El Grande sat forward on the chair with his arms and hands flat on the table. The letter said that the operation on La Grande's eyes had been done. The doctors didn't know if it had worked yet, but La Grande was in good spirits. El Grande smiled and thanked God for His mercy. My mother said that my sister Dolores, who now lived in Duke City and worked for the Zale's store, was very helpful. Without her, who knows what we would have done, she wrote. When my father read that he and El Grande should take good care of me and to tell me that she loved me, tears filled my eyes. She finished by saying that she could hardly wait for the three of us to come to the city. Suddenly, I missed my mother.

"¿Qué tienes, hombre?" El Grande asked, looking up at me and laughing.

"Leave me alone," I said quickly, trying to wipe the shame off my face.

"Respeto," my father scolded.

As my father looked through the rest of the mail, they talked about many other things.

"Now you don't have to work so hard. No horses and no cattle to worry about," my father said. El Grande didn't even look up. "I think you should sell the rancho," he added.

"The land is to be worked, not to be sold," El Grande said, with a little poison in his voice.

"You have all the money you will ever need. And if you sell the rancho, you might even have a little to give to me," my father said, laughing lightly.

"I want you to take what money is needed to pay the doctors. I am sure they have done their best. The rest, you can have it. I don't need it."

"No, Grande. All I want is for you to be at peace."

"Don't worry about me. I will be at peace. I want you to be sure about that."

With that, the talk around the table ended. My father stood up and announced it was time to find something to eat for supper. We had a house full of food. The trouble was finding it. We all went into the store and looked through some boxes. We found cans of applesauce, sardines, beans, horseshoes, tomato paste, baking powder, toothpaste, foot powder, and peanut butter. One of us said we should have sardines with mustard. Somebody else offered beans, salmon and applesauce. What do we do for bread? Luckily, somebody found a box of Alka-Seltzer. It was the first time all day that the three of us laughed. The more stuff we found the more confused we got and the more we laughed.

"Who knows how to cook?" I asked, worried.

"I can only cook if we build a fire outside," El Grande giggled.

"The gas pump will blow up," my father warned. "On the other hand, who cares?" We all laughed.

Finally we opened a can of salmon, then we made a sauce out of watered-down tomato paste. We ate it with peanut butter on crackers, Boston beans, and applesauce.

"Con buen hambre, no hay mal pan," El Grande said when it was all over, trying to restart some fun, but we were all a little queasy. We just sat at the table staring at nothing and hoping not to be the first to let go. I tried not to think about it. Instead, I thought about what life in the city was like. There were stores everywhere, movies, and even something called TV.

"We should go to Duke City for a little visit tomorrow, just like mother said in the letter," I said suddenly, looking at my father. He looked at me, then at El Grande. I could tell he had been thinking more or less the same thing.

"We are going for a long visit and it starts tomorrow. We have to take a load of things," my father announced.

"I cannot go to the city. I have much work to do up at the rancho. I still have the pigs, chickens, the dogs. No. I can't go. I can't go. I will help load the truck."

"But don't you want to see La Grande?" I asked.

"She is in good hands," El Grande assured. Then he turned to my father and pointed his hand at him as if to make sure he was listening. "You go to the city. There is no hope for you. The boy stays with me."

"You don't understand. We are all *moving* to the city. Flavio needs to go now so he can get used to the city, make friends, get ready for school there." My father was talking like a teacher now.

"The only school the boy needs is right here. He needs to be with me so I can give him the real education he needs. He is the last one. You have sent the other boys away. They are already ruined. A real education is learning the ways of the rancho, the mountains. How the corn grows. The land. How to butcher animals; they don't come in a tin can. A man must be able to read the wind, the sky, not all those books. I am old. When I am gone who will be left to do all these things?" El Grande's hand shook.

"Grande. The world has changed. Reading the wind is not important anymore. Reading fast is important. Writing in proper form is important. People now get paid to butcher animals. The boys are not ruined. They are working on their future. And it is different than yours. It is different than mine."

"I will stay!" I blurted out without even thinking. My heart was hurting for El Grande.

"See, Flavio wants to stay!" El Grande came off his chair.

"No! The boy goes!" My father came off his chair.

I was sure there was about to be a fight. I stayed in my chair.

"*¡Desgraciadamente!*" El Grande shook his fist. Then he sat back down before finishing whatever he had started to say. My father stood up and walked away from the table.

For what seemed like forever, my father stood at the opposite end of the room while El Grande sat at the table, his eyes looking down at the floor. I looked at each one of them, wondering who was going to make the next move. Time seemed to drag on, but nobody said anything more.

Finally, El Grande stood up. He headed slowly for the door, and as he opened it, he turned to me and said, "I will be here to say good-bye in the morning." He slowly closed the door behind him. My father didn't move.

The early morning sun was just barely peeking over Tío Samuel's house and already we had loaded the truck and were ready to go. I gassed up the old truck; my father checked all the tires. I wanted to go across the road to see what El Grande was doing, but my father said I should wait. He checked our load of boxes, then all the doors of the house, then the tires, again.

Finally El Grande came out of his house, wearing his new hat. He came across the road in his hurried, official walk. "I have come to give the proper send-off. I am completely in charge here now," he said, proudly. I was surprised that he did not seem mad or hurt. It seemed as if nothing had happened between them. But with the words they had the night before, I knew their fight was deep and forever. Being nice here was just part of being strong.

"Why don't you change your mind and come with us?" my father asked. El Grande didn't answer, as though he hadn't heard. "Well, where's your gun to make all of this official?" he added, trying to lift things a little.

"My rifle has done all it can. It is now retired, just like you." He did not know that I knew where it was. My father looked at me, forehead wrinkled, but my face was like stone.

"Well, Grande, we must go. I will be back in two or three weeks. If you need for me to come back sooner, here is an envelope with a stamp and the address. Just put it in the mailbox. You don't even have to write something." My father had thought of everything and I was kind of proud of him. I walked over to El Grande and put my arms around his big belly.

"I will be back to see you soon, too," I mumbled. I could feel the tears headed toward my eyes from somewhere I couldn't understand.

"Los hombres se aguantan, hijo," El Grande said in a stern voice. I held back the tears. Who would want to be seen crying two days in a row?

With the sun now giving the Capulín Valley its full face, my father and I drove away from the front of the store. El Grande stood on the same spot where the *gringo* had slapped his rifle away on the day that Luke Evans was murdered. Through the red cloud of *caliche* dust, I could see El Grande standing on the side of the road, waving good-bye. As I looked out the back window, El Grande got smaller and smaller and my life on the rancho got farther and farther away.

"He's a stubborn old fool," my father said to no one in particular. "He doesn't even know what is best for him. Or for you. He is stuck in the past. He just doesn't see that the world has changed."

"I don't think you understand him," I sassed back. "He's old, yes, but he knows something you don't know. He knows where he came from. Where he is going. He is free. Not free like the picture of the Statue of Liberty. But free like he doesn't need anybody for nothing. He never even had a job like you. He said that his *dignidad* is the most important thing he owns. I'll bet that the people in the city don't have any of that." I said these things without even thinking I was disrespectful.

My father just looked at the road and didn't say anything. He lit a cigar and the truck stank.

The long trip dragged on and my legs got cramped. I had to pee but I didn't dare ask him to stop—he seemed in a hurry. I just went deep into my own mind, mixed with a little sadness and a little hope. With every bump of the road, I was being taken farther away from Capulín. I did not realize then what it all really meant. In my father's smelly truck there was no ceremony for my passing to another world, forever.

DIECISIETE

It was a little place, but clean. Two bedrooms and an inside peepee. The kitchen had everything modern. And in the living room, there they were: the TV and the telephone. I didn't know it right then, but in no time I would know all about "The Little Rascals," "Dragnet," "The Hit Parade," "The $64,000 Question," and I would be calling all over town asking about what every kid needed—a bike. With a dime, I could ride the bus for hours, just looking at all the gas stations, stores, and places to eat. There was so much to read.

In just a few days I set out in the morning to look for wheels. Everybody had one. I had a Mason jar full of dimes and nickels which added up to $13.80, enough to head toward 4th Street and hop a bus. I sat at the very front so I could see out the windshield and told the driver I was looking for a used bike. I guess he liked me because he helped me look. After many blocks we came up to a secondhand store and there it was, the bike of my dreams. He stopped the bus, opened the door and let me out.

One tire was flat and I didn't know how to ride it, but I knew it had to be mine. The man said he wanted $15.00. I showed him my jar and said all I had was $13.80. The man smiled, but said he was sorry. Back at the Capulín Cash Store when people didn't have quite enough money, they just said, *"Ahi te pago,"* and that was good enough. But when I told the man I would bring the $1.20 just as soon as I could, he just shook his head. No $15.00, no bike. I couldn't believe the man didn't trust me. He didn't even know me! I went outside and sat on the curb trying to figure out what to do. Finally I went back inside, gave the man my jar full of money and asked him to keep it. I would be back for the bike as soon as I had $1.20. I started to walk out, but he called me back.

"Take the bike, kid. You can have it for $13.80 and there's a pump. Air up the tires," he said. He even helped me with the pump. When the tires were filled and I was the proud owner, he asked, "Do you know how to ride this thing?"

"No."

"Oh, my God." The man looked a little sick. "For Chris'sake, walk the damn thing home and don't get hit by a car. Your parents will have my ass if you get hit."

"Oh, no, sir. I'm sure they don't want it," I said *todo* naive.

I spent the next days learning to ride the bike. Jimmy, Billy, and Bobby lived on my street. They were brothers. They helped me learn. By the time I could ride up and down the street, the pedals were rubbing against the frame and I had gone through the knees of a new pair of Levi's.

Somehow I thought I would go back to Capulín and take my bike with me, but my mother informed me differently. I was going to school in Duke City and it started in two days. They were buying the little pink house and we were going to be city people. The entire rancho would be sold and the Grandes would come to the city. My brother Juan and my sister Cordy would finish at the boarding school and come. My brother Adrian was still in the U.S. Navy, but when he was done he would come to Duke City. We would be together, a happy family, I thought.

The school was bigger than Capulín. People everywhere. The long shiny halls were lined with lockers, big clocks stuck out of the walls everywhere, as though time was important. Almost all the kids were *gringos,* some with metal wires on their teeth. Everybody seemed to know everybody else. Those who didn't look like *gringos* thought they were. When I spoke Spanish to them, in serious need of quick friends, they just walked away. Suddenly I felt like what the *gringo* kids in Capulín must have felt. *¡Hijo!* Life is so tricky, I thought.

In a moment near tears, I spotted a person leaning against the wall who seemed as scared as I was. I didn't know exactly what kind of person he was, but he was as dark as Tío Mateo, so I figured he was good people. For sure, he was not a *gringo* kid.

"*¿Qué pasa?*" I said as I walked up to him, hoping finally for a friend.

"I doan talk dat stuff," he said quickly. "Ma name's Ernie... Ernie Coates," he said as he stuck his hand out. I shook his hand and told him my name. Without more words, we just turned and cruised down the hall as though we'd grown up together. From that day on, me and the first *Negro* person I had ever seen were *todo* cool in middle school.

I had never played football, but my brother Juan had played it at the boarding school, so I knew it was rough. But Ernie knew what it was all about. In just a few days before practice started, Ernie had taught me the main points. He was bigger and stronger than I, but I was faster. The years of chasing horses and getting away from La Aprovechada's flashing yellow teeth were about to pay off. When the tryouts came for the glory of playing for the Garfield Gophers, we were ready.

On the football field, we found the only other lost kid. His name was Tony Acoya, an Indian from the Acoma tribe. He was neither strong nor fast, but he had a knack. He was able to not be where you thought he was and appear where you thought he wasn't. When he ran with the ball, nobody could find him to tackle. Tony had only one problem. When he got excited, he couldn't talk. Unlike Ernie who talked so fast when he got excited that we couldn't understand him.

Football was almost as rough as breaking horses. *Patadas* everywhere. It was hot, dry, and we couldn't drink water until it was all over. In the locker room it smelled worse than the barn. Then there were the showers. I had just barely learned what a shower was and already I was in a room with thirty of them. Thirty guys would take a shower together, cleaning our bruises and bloody spots. It was also a chance to see how we compared.

After practice one late afternoon, the three of us were hanging around 4th Street waiting for the bus. Suddenly, we were in a fight with six big guys who jumped out of a car and came after us. They were wearing blue jackets that said FUTURE FARMERS OF AMERICA. I yelled that I was a farmer, too, but it didn't help. They beat us up and took off. We picked ourselves up from the weeds and checked to see if we had all our arms and legs still on. About that time, Tony started grunting and pointing to his left eye. It was gone!

"My glass eye—gone." He went down on his knees searching in the weeds. "If I don't find it my dad will kill me," he said.

I had never heard of a glass eye, but by now Tony was just cussing and saying, "Oh, shit."

We were all on our knees until dark, but no eye. Finally we promised Tony we would all come back in the morning and look some more.

The next day we didn't go to homeroom. The three of us went straight to see the principal.

"We would like permission to skip first period and go to 4th Street to look for Tony's eye," I asked as the Assistant Principal, Mrs. Hays. She looked at us a little disgusted, especially at Tony's empty socket. "We got jumped last night after practice. Tony lost his eye in the fight." She looked around to check if anybody else had heard what we wanted.

"Okay. But you must be back before the second bell for second period," she ordered.

In the light of the new day all five of our good eyes were in the weeds and Ernie soon came up with the one brown, glass eye. Tony was a happy man. He plunked it into his mouth to wash it and then popped it back into his face.

The secret of Tony's eye was out. During hall cruising, Tony would put his eye between his lips and teeth and wink at the girls with his mouth. They would scream and wrinkle their faces, disgusted. Everybody liked to see us coming down the hall. We were finally cool brown, red and black cats in the jungle of little white faces.

The three of us had English class together. Miss Arrechi was our teacher. She was built like those women in the Sears book. I was in love with her and always tried to do really good in English. But one day we were studying prepositions when Miss Arrechi came over to my desk in the front row, where I had been moved from Ernie and Tony to try to improve my attention.

"Would you tell the class what a preposition is," she said to me *toda* sexy. I tried to picture Mrs. Majors saying something about prepositions. I wanted to do good for my true love, Miss Arrechi.

"Yes. Well, ahh, a preposition is anything that a rabbit can do to a hole." I knew I had heard that somewhere.

The entire class was laughing. Ernie even fell off his desk and was howling on the floor.

What was so funny? I wondered.

Miss Arrechi calmed them down and told them what rude people they were. "Would you elaborate?" she said to me.

I almost didn't know what elaborate was. A few giggles were still around. "Well... you see, a rabbit can go around his hole, over it, by it, toward it, away from it, into it, and like that. You gotta know that when you hunt them," I said, ready for the next blast of laughs.

"That is excellent!" Miss Arrechi said with a big smile. "Class, now isn't that a clever paradigm?"

"What's a paradigm?" some kid asked.

"Oh, that's twenty cents, like two dimes," Ernie said with his little grin.

Everybody laughed again.

"Well, it looks like we are going to learn two important concepts today," Miss Arrechi said, and she went on to explain a paradigm.

I loved her! My star was lit. I worked harder in English than in any other class. For me, the word *excellent* became the thing to shoot for in school. I liked the word and I wanted more.

Life in the city soon became a part of me and it seemed I was always busy: football practice, homework, and my friends. The days had become shorter and I usually got home after dark, most of the time with a new bruise or a pain somewhere. It was starting to get cold, too, and all the leaves on the trees had turned red and yellow. The kids were already talking about the Halloween parties. But when it came to witches, they had nothing on me.

It was a breezy evening when I got home one particular day, hungry, tired, and aching. A new pickup was in the driveway. My sister's car was there. My uncle's old Plymouth was parked on the street. It looked like we were having a party, or something.

I went into the house through the back door, crossed the kitchen, and found a big group of people sitting in the little living room. Bernabé and Pedro were sitting on the couch. My uncle was there, my parents, La Grande, and my sisters. I said hello to everybody and went over and shook hands with Bernabé and Pedro. My mother started crying and La Grande had her face covered with a black cloth. My sister came to me and put her arms around me. She, too, started to cry.

"Hey, what's going on here?" I asked. I thought maybe I had done something really wrong and everybody was here for a little *consulta.*

"El Grande is dead," my sister said calmly as she held me in her arms. Bernabé and Pedro stood up, their hats in their hands. Through the tears quickly filling my eyes and my sister's hair, I could see all the blurred, sad faces across the room. The giant of my youth was gone.

DIECIOCHO

"At the moment that you are dying you are the most powerful," he had told me in one of his strange times. "Except for when you are born, it is the only time you are *completamente* alone; in charge." I had been with him in some powerful moments, as when the *rinches* caught us hunting bears and we got away, or when he told all the people of Capulín about the evil of electricity, or when he buried Rosa Velásquez. But dying? How could he do it without me? In my sadness, I wanted to die, too. And why wasn't I there with him, instead of playing football and messing around with Ernie and Tony? Then there was Miss Arrechi to feel bad about, too. I even wanted to marry her someday, as soon as I knew as much English as she did. *¡Sinvergüenza!*

Suddenly I was very mad at him for dying without me, for not telling me that was what he was going to do. During the long, dark night, I went from sad to mad and back to sad. And where was God in all of this? How come he didn't do anything to help?

In church they talked about heaven. I wondered if he had found it. I remembered one time I had asked him where he thought heaven really was. He had laughed at my question.

"God is with His heaven like the government is with its money," he said. "It has a whole mountain of it, but it never tells us where it is. If people knew where it was, they would spend all their time trying to get it. Who would do the work? Same thing with heaven." I was sure that he and Smokey, the wild paint, had found it.

The worst was the waiting. I helped my sister clean the house. I liked the vacuum because it worked like nothing I had ever seen before. I went all over the house, sucking up everything that wasn't tied down. Until word came about where the *velorio* was going to be, cleaning was a good way to rest my soul. I had heard La Grande say that she wanted to go to Capulín and bring him to the city. When people called on the telephone, my sister Dolores just told them to leave a number.

Finally, by the end of the next day my mother called from La Ventana saying that he was being brought to the city. They would be home late. She said to clean the house because a lot of people were coming. I asked my sister where we were going to put him. She laughed for the first time in many days. They would take him to a mortuary, she informed me. What did I know? In the rancho you just buried them quickly, before they started to smell.

I decided I would stay up and wait for my mother and father to come from Capulín, just in case they still had him. I wanted to see him. When the TV went off after the Stars and Stripes at midnight, they were still not home, so I fell asleep. In the early morning a racket in the kitchen woke me up. It was finally them. Sleepy and a little confused, I hugged my mother and asked to see the body. She said his body was already at the mortuary, but that he was with God. I felt good. So the wild paint pony from the *chamisal* had done his job, I thought.

The funeral service was at the church in a part of the city called Martíneztown. It was a very old church that looked like the Indian *pueblos,* but inside it had all the regular saints and

Jesus on the cross. It smelled a little like Mrs. Majors' school. The light of the bright day came through little windows way up high that showed angels or saints made of colored glass. The whole place made me feel like I really wanted to behave myself.

By the time me and the rest of the family got there, the place was almost full of people, hundreds of them. Relatives from far away, *gringos,* Indians from the Jicarilla. Some of them came in their leathers and feathers as they would dress for their sacred times.

Because we were *familia,* we got to sit toward the front, close to all the action. The casket was already there, up front where everybody could see it. It was made of nice brown-colored metal that looked like it was actually wood. The cover was open and you could see that the whole thing was lined with some kind of fine white cloth, maybe silk. I knew El Grande was in there, but I couldn't see him from where I was sitting. When I stretched a little I could see his nose and the top of his *pancho villa.*

After a lady with a beautiful voice sang a song with the organ playing, everyone was quiet, except for a few noses being blown around the church. Then entered the *Reverendo* Candelaria wearing a long black robe. He walked up to where the preacher always stood and asked everyone to pray with him. Reverendo Candelaria had nothing but good things to say about El Grande. I wondered if he even knew him, but I agreed with just about everything he had to say. He said that there are those who God puts right here in the world to inspire us, to show us how He wants us all to behave.

"Don Ezequiel was among those few whose soul, in all its being, was dedicated to goodness in the world. He lived his life as an example for mankind. He was a giant among men." The preacher looked around the church as though ready to point a few fingers. "And now God has called him to His kingdom to do a greater good, among the angels in heaven." He said this should not just be a sad time for us; that we should celebrate his life, his having lived among us.

"God works in mysterious ways. He gives when we do not realize He is giving and He takes in the same way." The *reverendo* paused to let it all sink in. People seemed to be saying 'yes' with their heads. I *absolutamente* agreed with him that God works in funny ways. Many times I had asked God for a little favor here and there and as far as I could tell, He only worked now and then. Now I realized that He probably had answered all my prayers, but I didn't even know when He had done it.

"He leaves family, friends, and many lives he has touched." Reverend Candelaria began to finish his sermon. He turned toward us, where all the *familia* was seated. "In your grief you, his family, have much to rejoice on this day. He shared with you, his wisdom, his kindness and his understanding of the world around us. But his world is now gone and it is you who must carry on. It is you who now carry his vision and his message. He lives through you. God bless you."

All was quiet.

I felt like standing up on the seat and yelling, "I'll do it! I'll do it! I will be just like him." But even now I thought of the reata and that El Grande might give me a little heavenly swat for not behaving in church. Instead, I let a few little tears come out of my already blurry eyes. The organ started playing. The woman with the beautiful voice sang "Rock of Ages," a song that I had heard my mother hum many times while she was busy doing work around the store.

When the service was over, everybody passed by the front of the church where the open casket with white lining sat. I wasn't sure if I wanted to go and look, too, but the crowd didn't give me any choice. I walked up to the front and looked in. It was the first time I had seen him since the day he had waved good-bye on the side of the dusty road. He was wearing his black suit, the one he always wore for special times: marriages, Easter, the last night of *luminarias,* the night when the *acequia* was finished, funerals. Now he was wearing it for his own. His face had a look of calm, as he had always looked when things were just right, *satisfecho.* I had seen that face many times, and through my tears I was happy to see that he was happy, too. I reached up and touched his hard chest, then his cold face. I knew then that his soul was with God. I knew he couldn't hear me, but I told him I loved him anyway.

People headed for their cars, trucks, some even hitched a ride. I got to ride in a beautiful, long, *todo* fancy Cadillac because I was *familia.* Even the police were helping with the long line of cars. If El Grande could have seen it, he would have thought the *rinches* had changed their minds about him, I thought. The long line passed through the gates of Sunset Memorial and wound around to where there was an open grave, ready for the eternal resident. People gathered all around, close *familia* getting to sit in the few chairs provided by the owners, no doubt. There *Reverendo* Candelaria had a few more good things to say, but by that time everybody knew El Grande could do no wrong. People picked up a little pinch of dirt and threw it in the grave after the casket was sent down with fancy ropes. It was tradition.

El Grande had finally reached his final resting place, in Sunset Memorial Park, Duke City.

Hundreds of people gathered at our little pink house. The smell of good food was all over the neighborhood: Beans, *chile, carne asada,* tortillas, rice, *sopa de pan,* and here and there, a few beers. I finally got to say hello to George, Tusa, and all the other guys from Capulín. Everybody was talking at once. *Compadres* were telling each other how long it had been, and *comadres* were giving each other advice about everything. Hugs and tears every now and then. Out in the back yard most of the men were standing around. Somebody had lit a fire in the big steel barrel we used to burn leaves. In the cool of the afternoon, it was good to have a little heat. The men stood around it just like the potbelly back at the Capulín Cash

Store. They talked about everything, important and unimportant.

Pedro talked about the oil wells being drilled up on the French Mesa, where they said there was more oil than all the cars and trucks in the state could burn in a hundred years. Roads had been punched into the deep canyons where once only long trips on horses could get you to where the very big bucks hid. Now you could drive up there and shoot them from the truck. Somebody else wondered how Torpe Molina had been able to escape from the Tierra Amarilla jail and where he might be hiding. Roberto said that he had heard that Torpe had dressed up like a chicken and was living in the oak thicket. Everybody laughed. The Indian, El Mocho, said that he had finally decided that killing Luke Evans was a bad thing to do; that Torpe deserved to live like a chicken, eating his own *huevos* for the rest of his life. He was happy that now everybody got along so good. The baseball games got around; how the Capulín team had finally beaten the *gringos* and what a fiesta it had been, with the *gringos* paying for all the beer.

As I listened to all the men from Capulín, I began to understand what the power of dying was. You are the most powerful then, and it lasts even after you have finished, I thought. Look at all the people he brought to this one place. People I didn't even know. All of Capulín. Not even the *eléctricos* with their bright lights could do that. *Gringos,* Indians, old, young, enemies, everybody there for the same thing: El Grande's death.

Word came from the kitchen. The food was ready. Paper plates, a modern thing from the city, were filled with beans, *chile,* rice, corn, carrot salad, tortillas and different sliced breads just in case you were not total *raza.* Soda, beer or wine, no matter what, it was there. I think I even spotted a little Hill & Hill. There was one more message from Our Maker by my sister Dolores, who had a little more religion than the rest of the family. She spoke of love and friendship; how we were all created equal, just like it goes with the Pledge of Allegiance. Then she ran down the list of wonders El Grande had done while here on the earth. Finally, she asked God to forgive all sins, and I could tell everybody was for that. *Al fin,* after the food was half-cold and people were starting to wiggle, she said 'Amen.'

"Con permiso," came a deep voice out of nowhere. It was El Mocho. "The dead one is now with the great spirit. In the end he decided to go with his Indian side. We have welcomed him into our house. He is with the ancestors. Now he has his own bearskin blanket. I was sent to give you this good news."

For a while, nobody moved. Then Malvino shuffled forward from the group of men. He made a grunting noise like a horse and stood stiffly. His eyes shifted from side to side as if making sure everybody was listening. Then he turned and stared at El Mocho of the Jicarilla. No one in the room seemed to breathe.

"Don Ezequiel is not dead. He lives. He lives but you cannot see him. Only I can see him. He lives with the animals of the forest. In the trees, the grass, the land. I know he is there. I speak with him. Now it is time to eat."

People looked at each other. Some mumbled things that were not kind. But La Grande thanked him and asked everyone to start with the food.

Our *gringo* neighbors found every reason to walk up and down the street, as if there was business to do at both ends of dead-end Gene Avenue. Peeks into the back yard, where the men burned their plates in the rusty barrel after they finished eating, were the main event of the street cruise. Little kids came up the driveway to stare. I wondered what they thought: Who are all these people of different colors, talking strange languages, eating all this smelly food, some laughing and some crying? I was sure they were not used to our kind of funeral in this neighborhood.

It is interesting how good food and a few *traguitos* of something cold will loosen up the tongue. Everybody had a favorite memory about El Grande: the potato harvests; the *acequia,* the winter of '51, the burial of Rosa Velásquez and the fireball, and the escape from the rinches after a bear hunt.

Then Bernabé started in a low voice. *"Pues,* early one morning on my way to work, Malvino stopped me at the turnoff to the *molino.* He was yelling and screaming. He was saying take me to the top of the mountain, something is wrong. What do you do when you are not yet *completamente* awake and a wild, crazy man is screaming at you from the side of the road? I took him. When we got to the top of the mountain, Malvino told me to take this road and then that one, like he had already been there. The dusty roads all looked the same to me, but he knew. We finally got near some *lagunitas* where we spotted a *pinto* grazing down in a little meadow. We stopped. Malvino jumped out of my truck. I followed him up the hill, through a thick *encinal.* We finally came to a clearing. He was bug-eyed and crazy-looking. We ran all around the clearing, all the time Malvino looking for tracks like he was the great hunter that you all know he isn't. Finally we came out from behind some bushes and there, sitting against a tree, looking far across the canyon of the Río Chama toward the Mesa de Las Viejas, we found the old man. He was dead." Bernabé choked.

For a while he said no more. The men stood frozen around the barrel, as though they had never heard this story before.

"He was stiff. I touched him. Don Ezequiel was dead. How Malvino knew? I don't know."

Nobody moved.

When Bernabé finally spoke again, he said how the family had been called to claim the body, by this time El Grande lying peaceful on top of the new pool table at the Capulín Bar. Malvino kept saying that he must be taken back to the *lagunitas* and buried near some Indian ruins. That he belonged there. He said he had had a vision. That the old man was a gift of the high mesas and he must be returned there. "Lucky everybody knows what a crazy man he is. You heard him in there," he said in a hushed voice. They all laughed a little and a bottle of Hill & Hill started making its way around the barrel. The men were celebrating just like the *reverendo* had said we should.

I knew. I knew what nobody else knew. Malvino was right. El Grande had gone there to be with his mountain, with all his old friends: all the ancient Indians, like Antigua. The dead Indians were all he had left, but were better for him than anything still walking around, I thought. I wanted to go over near the smoking barrel and tell the men everything. I wanted to tell them that Malvino was right. The old man did belong in the mountain; Malvino's vision was true. I wanted to tell them that Malvino wasn't crazy as everybody had always believed. El Grande had said he would die with dignity and honor. What better dignity? I couldn't tell them. They would think I was crazy, too.

I sat down on the damp dirt and leaned back against the wall between our yard and our neighbor, Mr. Ridner's. The men's talk kept on getting louder as the Hill & Hill made the rounds, but I did not listen anymore. I had heard everything I wanted to hear.

El Grande's body was now deep in the ground at beautiful Sunset Memorial burial grounds, but his soul was on top of his mountain.

PARTE TRES

Vision

DIECINUEVE

It would take several days to rid my system of the acute effects of the drugs after every treatment. When the awful taste of *Adriamycin* in my mouth was gone, I knew that the retching would soon subside. In the meantime, the oncologist who had treated me had somewhat sheepishly recommended that I try to find a connection to some marijuana, because of its medical value in controlling extreme nausea. He was a very proper and professional physician to whom you could never get very close. Perhaps it was his way of guarding himself from the constant pain of people dying while under his care and the frustration of not being able to do any more for them. Whatever his personality faults may have been, he certainly knew his business, even about the marijuana. When the nausea would grip me with an exhausting and unrelenting hold, I would take a few hits. The effects were nearly immediate the nausea would subside and I would pick up a few hours of much needed sleep.

It was several days after my last treatment, a process that had taken over a year. The excitement of being alive and able to drive again was almost too much to believe. I stomped on the gas pedal and headed south on the interstate on a mission I had long intended to make and one for which I had almost lost the opportunity. It was early in the morning, long before my staff would begin arriving at the office. My plans were to try and reach Taos by late afternoon and spend the night there. Since it was late spring, the days were already long, so I knew that with a little luck I would be able to catch a glimpse of the Cerro del Pedernal, visible from a point near Taos, far off in the southwestern horizon just before sunset. Somehow it seemed a fitting goal for the first day of my long-awaited return to the land of *poco tiempo.*

Even for a weekday, Taos was overrun by tourists. The old plaza was full of people, mostly Anglos and leftover hippies. Finding a hotel room was impossible, so I drove down the canyon and camped out along the Rio Grande not far from its confluence with Dixon Creek. I spent the rest of the afternoon and into the evening exploring all the little back roads. I returned to my little campsite well after dark. After eating some dried fruit and cheese and gulping down some protein supplements I was taking to help bring my weight back up from the ninety-eight pound weakling I had become, I crawled into my sleeping bag in the back of the truck. The monotony of the river against the stillness of the night, the smells of juniper, *chamiso* and *piñón,* and the pulsating sounds of the traffic up on the highway all combined to lull me to a restful sleep.

Morning came quickly. After coffee and gas at the local cash and carry, I drove down the canyon until I picked up the road to Chama. In another hour I came to the junction with State Road 96 and headed southeast. I was headed to the bank of the Abiquiu Dam, built across the Rio Chama by the Army Corp of Engineers to control floods and silt. Through the rearview mirror, I could see the colorful red sandstone cliffs near Ghost Ranch. Brightly lighted by the early morning sun and dead ahead was the majestic profile of the Cerro del Pedernal, now rising from the prairie floor like a giant cone fashioned by an ancient rupture of the earth. The new highway no longer followed the old route up the *cuesta del puerto,* so it wasn't long before I reached the upper edge of the Capulín Valley. Coming over the top of a low hill and rounding a gentle curve, the valley suddenly opened in front of me like fresh blossoms of the vivid memories that had been planted so long ago. I pulled over to the side of the road at a spot where I had a clear view of the valley and far beyond it to where the French Mesa met the horizon. Through my field glasses I could see the signs of renewal everywhere: Newborn calves sleeping in groups of three or four, vast fields of dandelions surrounded by the light-green grass of spring, and a young colt running with an outstretched tail in a sweeping circle around its mother. Somewhere in the distance, unseen from where I stood, the low drone of a tractor gave me the first clue of human presence.

From there on I drove slowly, allowing every detail to reconfirm all that was stored in me. Down the road, I met a pickup truck on the highway. The driver waved as he passed, just like "down-home" folks always do. A few miles into the valley I came upon a fellow who had pulled off the side of the road and was standing near his pickup. As I came up to him he waved at me to stop. I could see he had a flat tire, and two kids in the truck. I could also see his left leg had been amputated above the knee. He hobbled over on his metal crutches and asked if I had a jack he could borrow. I could immediately tell it was José Torres, a grown-up version of the obnoxious toothy kid I had once known. I told him I had a small hydraulic jack that would probably do the job fine. In a few minutes we had the front of his truck up on the jack, ready to put on the spare.

"Hey. I see you're from out of state, *amigo,*" he said as he tightened the lug nuts on his wheel.

"Yup. Just passing through," I said, sure he had not recognized me. I didn't tell him who I was. This trip into deep memories, into a search for a new vision, could not be complicated by the recovery of old social ties. I wanted it to be pure.

"Chure glad you come along; not much traffic on dis road dese days." He spit a big glob of tobacco juice as he paused. "Was gettin ready to send my boys here down over the hill to borrow a damn jack from Sánchez. A flat tire and one leg don't leave a lot of choice, if you know what I mean."

"Hell of a thing to have to get by on one leg," I agreed.

"Vietnam," he said as he looked up at me. "Some goddam little Chinaman planted a mine in the stinky jungle just for me. Wish I could get my hands on the *hijo de la chingada.* I would rip his guts open with this lug wrench and feed them to the dogs."

I felt for him, but what really grabbed me was how much he still sounded like José Torres, the sixth-grade kid. We chatted on for a few more minutes after the job was done.

"Llega a mi chante. Nos echamos unas frías," he said, now facing me straight as he balanced on one crutch, with his lug wrench in the other hand. It was a sad José Torres who was asking me to stop by his place for a few beers. I said that I wished I could but I had to get moving. I would stop at some other time, when I came by this way again. He shook my hand and thanked me for the help.

I headed on down the road again, confirming that I was indeed in the midst of whatever was left of Capulín. I could see that a few farmers were making the early efforts to get the soil ready for the year's crop, or fixing fences which had fallen during the winter. After several miles I rolled up to a forest service sign that read MESA ALTA, with an arrow pointing to the right. This was it, the turn that put me on the old logging road, up the *cañoncito* and onto the mesa where the fence line of the old rancho was now just a tangle of barbed wire and an occasional fence post.

The winter snow was almost all gone, except on the north-facing slopes where the spring sun shines late; *sombrillos,* as El Grande used to call them. In some places big mud puddles made the going rough, even in four-wheel drive. Winding my way along the edge of the old familiar aspen grove and up a low hill I came to where the potato patch had once been. It was now covered with tall weeds and chest-high pine saplings. Next came the meadow, full of yellow dandelions, and beyond it the slope where the cabin had stood. All that was left of it were parts of three walls and a section of the porch where Antigua had once scared the hell out of me. I did not stop. It was getting close to sunset and I wanted to reach my final destination before nightfall.

Tall, billowing thunderheads toward the west threatened rain for the coming night, so I knew I had to move fast. After a few more miles on the logging road which was now not much more than a trail, I arrived in my mud-splattered truck at the *lagunitas*. It was an awesome sight. The setting sun sent rays of pink, red, and purple light halfway across the sky. Off to the left, bolts of lightning lit up the puffy clouds and the thunder shook the ground as it rolled across the mountain. Out at the horizon, the gray silhouette of la Mesa de Las Viejas descended to the now dark canyon of the Rio Chama, straight down from where I stood. The chilly wind blew through the tall pine forest making the hollow sounds of a distant waterfall.

Standing where El Grande and I had spent that dreadful night so many years before, I felt at once the power, the fear and the magic of the spot. I felt a strange sense of excitement. It was as if I had managed to step into the past. I was a child again.

I gathered wood, built a fire, and sat down to eat the last of my cheese and fruit. I also finished off the awful protein drink. In a loud voice I told myself how beautiful the sunset had been and how enchanting the evening that was descending upon me was. The black clouds with millions of stars peeking around them; the play of lightning bright enough to power thousands of traffic lights; the air so clean it could send your lungs into shock; and so alone that no matter how loud I screamed, no human would hear me.

The night closed in on me. I fed the fire. The canyon of the Chama filled with clouds and a massive storm of lightning, thunder, and rain developed below me. Between thunderclaps I could hear the coyotes howling and arguing with each other. Owls up on the trees broke in to say they were present. In the bushes I could hear little animals moving about. I was alone, yet all around me there was noise, movement, life. I wondered how many pairs of eyes were, at that very moment, looking at me from the darkness. I recalled the day El Grande butchered my lamb, Perro, and the dream I had in which the animals of the forest came to tell me about the fire the *abuelo* had set. Would they come out of the darkness now to visit with me around the fire? I remembered my first winter bear hunt, and my last, how the old man had made me wriggle into the bear's den to tie a rope on the dead bear. I thought of the day the timber marker arrived to begin marking the trees to be cut for the sawmill and how El Grande could not stand to see his forest chopped down. I remembered the agony of my decision to go to the baseball games instead of having him teach me about the sacred slopes of the Pedernal.

As the memories paraded before me, I suddenly shifted to the thought that within a few feet from where I was sitting, El Grande's hex-barrel Winchester was being slowly reclaimed by the forest floor. He, too, must have sat there, alone with his thoughts, on the day the Almighty came to claim his soul. I had resisted the thought all evening, perhaps trying not to overload my mind with more than I could handle at one time. But now, as the hellacious storm reached the top of the mesa, everything struck at once: The loneliness, the fear; the rain; the cold; the power of the mountain. I jumped to my feet and ran to the truck, already wet and shivering from cold *and* fear. I quickly took my clothes off, unrolled my sleeping bag and crawled into it in the back of the Bronco. Rain and hail pelted the metal top and, although I covered my head with the thick down bag, I could still see the nearly constant light of the electrical storm. As the air in my nostrils warmed a bit, I became convinced I smelled raw gasoline fumes. Could I have ruptured a fuel line on my way in? What if my gas leaked out and I couldn't get out? Worse yet, what if lightning struck nearby? I would fry!

"What am I doing way up here by myself?" I asked out loud. "Even if I am lucky enough to survive the night, the road will be impassible. Is this the ultimate design? Will I die here, too?" I bargained with the spirit of the mountain. "I have worked hard all my life. I have not been a religious person, but I am not evil. I have stood tough against the big C. I have chosen a career to help my fellow man. I have even considered becoming an environmentalist. I'll make you a deal. If you let me out of here alive I'll go to church regularly... and I'll join the Sierra Club. And I'll never come back to bother you again."

I lay there for an eternity with my eyes wide open waiting for an answer. I thought of the ways it could possibly come: I could be hit by lightning and just explode; one last surviving grizzly could punch through the window and take me out; Antigua could rise out of the ground nearby and come over and shoot me with the Winchester; or, I could be spared and nothing would happen.

"What crazy thoughts," I complained. "Enough! *¿Qué chinga'os tienes?*" I asked myself. "The old man would be real proud of you, candy-ass." I composed myself. I began to relax. "If my number is up, it's up."

Close to midnight the rain finally quit and the wind died down. I could still hear the thunder, but it was now far away. I rolled over in my sleeping bag, avoiding a few bolts that stuck out of the floor and tried to go to sleep. I finally did.

It was a brilliant morning. The sun was breaking through the clouds and the trees cast long shadows over the edge of the mountain. Everything was wet and fresh. Here and there little rivulets were still flowing. The blue jays were having their usual spats and the tree squirrels moved busily from branch to branch. The canyon of the Chama was now quickly filling with light, and the mesa beyond looked so much closer than the evening before. In such a beautiful morning I walked around filled with energy, finding the exact spot where Antigua and the rifle were buried and where El Grande must have dug for artifacts in the old ruins. So many years had passed yet everything looked the same, as if time had stood still. I dared not disturb anything. I had made a deal the night before.

Having found no gas leak, I started the truck and let it warm up for a few minutes. I turned the front wheel hubs to lock them in four-wheel drive and took one last look down into the canyon. I was now ready to drive away from the mountain. At times the Bronco sank all the way down to the axles as I drove in the mud, and in most places it was easier going on the grass, off the old road.

By the time I arrived at the paved road it was midmorning. I stopped and cleaned the mud off the windshield and the license plate. You could not even tell the color of the truck with the mud, but I was now ready to head into the lower valley.

State Road 96 had been re-routed and paved sometime during the past twenty-five years. When I arrived at the unmarked junction with the dirt road to the *molino,* I veered right and headed toward the old sawmill, my head filled with curiosity. The road was where it had always been but heavily scarred with the ruts of winter travel without maintenance. I went by the spot where the *gringos'* baseball field had once stood and approached the main drag of the *molino* community. Empty hulks of lumber houses in neat rows suddenly emerged from the now overgrown *chamisos* to tell me that the heyday of boardfoot production had long since passed. The main area where the huge radial saws once bit into an endless stream of ponderosa and fir logs had burned down. Nearby, several huge metal tanks that fueled the works lay rusting under the bright sun. Already new saplings of the surrounding forest grew along the rotting timbers.

I parked the truck and walked up near the ruin. In my memory I could hear the shrill whine of the saws ripping through green pine. I could see the billowing cloud of smoke from the scrap burner. The penetrating smell of fresh wood mixed with the aroma of diesel fuel filled my senses. Had the witch, Rosa Velásquez, in the form of a coyote, been granted a childhood request to burn the place down? Had the great Creator punished the *gringos* for getting El Grande drunk? Or had the Duke City Lumber Corporation simply used up the vast riches of the deep forest and merely moved on to another place, leaving the cleanup to vandals and time? Perhaps it didn't really make any difference now. The forces of nature were indeed slowly healing the wounds.

I headed back down the road toward the paved highway feeling a sense of completion, now able to close a small but important window to the past. As I came to the junction, I spotted an old man sitting on the ground next to a group of mailboxes. At first I did not recognize him, but old as he looked, I figured he had a story I should hear. I parked my truck on the opposite side of the road and walked over to where the man greeted me with a warm, toothless smile and a gesture toward a large rock where I could sit. He looked like an old man; bent, weathered; what was left of the hair on his head was fully gray. Against the backdrop of red *caliche* clay and the clumps of juniper that grew nearby, as if to frame him in silvery green, he radiated an official presence. Cataracts on both eyes told of his failing sight, so I knew he could not know who I was. But there was no doubt on my part, Malvino had managed to become an old man at a time when most of his contemporaries were struggling with middle age.

I sat on the rock next to him and leaned back against the roadbank. For several moments neither one of us said anything.

"*¿Que no chupas?*" he finally asked in a tone suggesting he already knew my answer. I said I didn't smoke and apologized for not having any cigarettes, but I offered him a stick of

Doublemint. As he mouthed the gum between his toothless jaws, I tried to start a conversation. I pointed out how nice the green grass looked among the sagebrush out on the slopes. He nodded in agreement. After a couple more attempts to get him talking with no success I decided to be more direct.

"Are there any jobs around here?" I asked in Spanish.

"You are not from around here, eh?" He chuckled as he spoke.

"I've been living up north for quite a while," I answered.

"When the *molino* burned down, everything stopped around here," he began as he repositioned his butt on the ground. With almost no trace of a once-disordered mind, he went on to explain how most of the *gringos* had moved out first. Then many others from Capulín moved out, too, in search of work. Many had gone to work in the atomic bomb "factory" at Los Alamos where it was said they were building another big one, this time for the Russians. He told of how people had practically given away their land; how some had left their families to look for work and had never come back. A few who stayed found work with the *floresta*. Several others worked for the Johnson Cattle Company. Johnson had come and bought the people's cheap land, or merely paid the taxes on abandoned parcels. He laid claim to all the forest grazing permits that the people were no longer using. Since the floresta would not issue any new ones, Johnson had exclusive rights to the public grazing lands all around Capulín. He also diverted the Capulín Creek onto his land for irrigation, and with what was left he filled a nice lake where he raised trout and charged tourists a fee to catch them. Thus, he built his cattle-ranching operation and his power. Nothing could happen in Capulín without his permission. The people complained, but little happened.

"Then one day there came a revolutionary named Trementina who explained to them that the public lands actually belonged to them under provisions set forth in an old land grant from the king of Spain. They filed their case in court many times, but each time the judge found reasons why it could not be heard. Finally the people got fed up, armed themselves and prepared for war. They bought new rifles, pistols, and plenty of ammunition. Then they blocked all the roads that led to the national forest and claimed it as their own. They declared the national forest as the new nation of Aztlan. They also got ready for an invasion of the county seat. On the day the citizens attacked Tierra Amarilla, Johnson had alerted the U.S. Army. The people's army was no match for the machine guns and tanks. The battle lasted only a few minutes before they had to surrender. Then there was a big trial, finally. The court decided the people had no case and Trementina was put in prison for starting the war. Now the government sends us all a check every month to keep us quiet.

"*¿Que no tienes más chíquete?*" Malvino asked as he brushed his brow. I handed him another stick of gum which he added to the first. Then he continued. "A long time ago this valley was the nest for our soul. Around the bend and down a bit lived the man the good Lord selected to take care of it. He was in charge: of reason, respect, and good will. When one of us died he was in charge of sending the soul to the Creator, and when a new one was born he added one back. He was the mayordomo of the acequia which the people used to water their beans and corn. Nobody went hungry. And nobody needed a free check from the government. The young respected the old and they did not smoke the marijuana the way they do now."

I handed Malvino one more stick of gum which he slowly unwrapped and stuffed into his mouth. I told him I was very interested in his story and to please keep going. He was giving me all I could have hoped for.

"Then one day, for reasons only I had the power to know, the bad will of God came down on our village. The foreign mind came. It was the same one that had come to the Mesa de Los Alamos to build *la atómica.* It came with a strange tongue, electric wires, big yellow machines and lots of money.

It blinded our eyes with dollars. The Keeper tried to warn the people, but they would not listen. He tried to fight it alone, but it was too strong even for him. He finally retreated to the bosom of the mountains, but the alien followed him. It ripped into the forest like a hungry monster. Finally the keeper outwitted it with the last thing he had left. He appealed to the Spirits of the mountain. And they answered with the only weapon that conquers all—Time.

"Now I sit here, day after day, and watch as its army slowly marches by. I no longer have many of my powers of vision and I will not be here for the final victory, but I know it will come." Tears rolled down Malvino's weathered face.

I put my arm around his bent shoulders and told him that I thought he was right. That I knew he was right!

Malvino and I drove around the bend where the *monte* came down to the edge of the highway. There I turned off the paved road and took the dirt road that passed in front of the houses that had been my home. Someone's laundry waved gently from wires strung across the porch of the old store. The hand-cranked gas pump was no longer there. A tall TV antenna doubled as a perch for a flock of sparrows. Across the road the house looked run-down, but colorful curtains covered the windows. In the courtyard, between the house and the old toolshed, someone's children were learning to ride a Honda minibike. A derelict truck sat rusting just beyond the hanging tree. I did not stop.

We drove to the top of the hill on the opposite side of the valley where the new consolidated school now stood. A little farther down the road, I turned on to a driveway and pulled up in front of an Exxon station. The place was also a little general store and the post office. A cheerful man came out to greet us.

"Hadidusa."

"How do you do, sir," I answered. "Pretty proud of your gas," I said, jabbing the guy a little.

"It's those damn A-rabs. They're goin'ta drive us to the poorhouse," he said, shaking his head. "How are you, Malvino?" he hollered as he stretched his neck to look inside the truck. Malvino did not answer. He just got down slowly and followed me into the store.

"¿Quiers una soda?" I asked as I pointed to the Coke machine.

"Y más chíquete," he answered with a big smile. I bought him a Coke and gave him my last stick of gum. As I wandered about inside the little store I spotted a beautiful nickel-plated potbelly stove set up in one corner. It was clear that someone had taken a lot of care in restoring the stove to its original condition. Even the top ornament was highly polished and properly turned so as to show off its fine detail.

"That'll be twenty-seven eighty," the attendant said as he entered the store wiping his hands with a rag. "Oal's okay."

"Christ! Why don't you just take my truck and give me a horse," I complained. He just laughed.

"From the looks of it you'd have a mighty long ride." He pointed over his shoulder with his thumb at my truck. "What brings you out these parts? Relatives, I bet."

"Naw. Just came out here looking for a friend," I said as I gestured toward Malvino. "Say, that's a fine stove you have over in the corner."

"Yeah." He smiled like a proud parent.

"You interested in selling it?"

"Don't think so. That there stove has a long story 'round these parts."

"I'd like to hear it if you have the time."

"Shore, plenny of time." He took a few moments to light a cigarette and also gave one to Malvino. "Well, down the bottom of the hill was a general store long time ago. That's when there waz nothing but Mexicans 'round here. The big landowner in the valley was the father of the owner's wife. He lived just across the road. Anything that happened in the village had to go through the ole man, kinda like Johnson is now.

This stove sat dab-splat in the middle of the little store. Winter or summer people gathered 'round it to take orders from the ole man. I say old 'cause he was already old when I was a kid 'n best friends to one of his grandsons. In fact he gave me the nickname I still go by locally here. Ennyways, this stove sat in there for years and years after the people moved away up to Duke City. Finally, when this fella Lorenzo Molina moved in there he just throwed it out back ta git it out of the way. So one day I just backed my pickup up to it and brung it home, dirty, rusty and full of stories. Spent big bucks gittin it re-plated and sporty like it is now. And there it sits. Don't hardly light it so as not to mess it up."

"What ever happened to the old man?"

"He refused to move to the city. The family couldn't blast him out 'a here. Tough ole cuss. People still talk 'bout him, you know, remember things he said and done. I always remember how he made me eat the first set of calf balls I ever ate. Tasted pretty good as I recall. Well, to make a long story short, one day the ole fool wandered up to the high country, got lost and pro'bly froze to death. I shore liked that ole man. Was kinda like a grandfather to me."

"What about his rifle?"

"Nobody knows. Just disappeared. Kinda like a mystery 'round these parts. Someday it might turn up. Hope it never does though."

"Why not?"

"Cuz it's so full of history, it would make ma stove seem like it wuz brand-new," he laughed. "Say, wait a minute. How'd you know 'bout the gun?"

"Well, I... ah, just figured a guy like that would leave more than one shrine." He looked me over carefully, like he knew I wasn't leveling with him. I looked back at him. "Sure you won't sell it."

"No way. It's part o'my roots. By the way, my name's Alvin," he said as he reached for my hand. We shook.

"Pleased to meet you, Alvin." I told him a name and for an instant I didn't know what else to say to him. "Well, you hang on to those roots. They're what keeps you sane, you know." Why argue? He was still here. He had earned it, I figured.

"Shore as hell will. You have a good trip, 'n I'll keep Malo, as we call him, here to keep me company for the afternoon."

I shook hands with both of them, climbed into the truck and headed back up the road. At the top of the hill overlooking the valley I pulled off to the side of the road and stopped for one last look.

It was spring and all was recovering from the cold of winter. Shades of green formed the backdrop for blotches of red, white and gold flowers across the valley floor. The willow and chokecherry thickets were on the verge of a new season, with delicate hues about to burst into full bloom. A flood of memories filled by mind, the warm afternoon sun on my face. I looked left, where the *molino* had once stood, and realized that the coyote had granted my childhood wish. The ball diamond, pride of *gringo* baseball, had also been reclaimed by the *chamisal*.

I thought of my encounter with José Torres, the lone sixth grader, and how the tragedy of Vietnam, like the atomic bomb, had not spared my village of Capulín.

I recalled Mrs. Majors and her thunderclap voice and all the things she had taught me, which I used every day—even fractions.

I remembered Tusa as the *vaquero* kid, and now he was the postmaster and the owner of the potbelly stove.

Then there was Malvino. Though he was probably schizophrenic and had suffered from this mental disorder since his youth, he had been a keen observer of all that happened in Capulín. In his own, often distorted perception of events, he had had uncanny insight.

The conflicts that had smoldered between my father and El Grande came to mind. The last of them over the move to the city. My education. My father had won both, eventually. Or had he?

The parade of memories and the nap that followed had taken what was left of the afternoon, and the sun was now resting on the farthest mesa. My thoughts returned to where I was and what I had become. How I had come so close to dying. The surgery. The chemotherapy. How I had reached that moment of power which El Grande had described so long ago. I, too, had seen that bright light at the end of the tunnel. I remembered vividly how I had made a conscious decision not to enter. Now, in this place of power, that vision returned. I saw him at the other end of the light calling to me. His figure was bright and translucent. His mood seemed urgent, questioning.

"I have a long time before I can enter. My children are young and my life's work is not yet done. My body is frail. I have come here to where you are to gain new strength. To touch the place where your soul lives.

"Much has changed, yet it is the same. The war against progress was fought and lost here. But your valley is in good hands. There is a continuity to all of this which we seldom see. Only those who have earned the vision can see it. I have seen but the first light. But now I understand. You had seen it in its fullest."

I looked around, hoping no one had seen me talking to myself as I sat on the rocks overlooking the valley of the Capulín.

In a few moments I walked back to the muddy Bronco and drove back up the paved highway in the direction I had come. And the Spirits of the High Mesa took the sun in, one more night.